THE FREE WORLD WAR II

A Probability of Evil

MATTHEW WILLIAM FREND

AUTHOR'S NOTE

The Free World War II – A Probability of Evil continues the story of a struggle to end the ceaseless and crippling arms races between opposing ideologies, and of a war to finally liberate humanity from the madness of perpetual conflict.

As with the first book in the series, our own tragic history is depicted from the viewpoint of a peaceful utopia that uses simulations generated with the aid of the limitless computing power and artificial intelligence of the future.

Conversely, the main storyline in which General George S. Patton survived his car accident, continues to describe the events of a war against global communism, a path which ironically may be the only way for us to achieve a utopian human society based on trust and an absence of fear.

FORWARD

There was a need to follow the first book in the Free World War series, not merely to continue a saga which compared an alternative human world to our own dysfunctional global civilisation, but to delve deeper into the causes of the horrific insanity of our past.

While researching the atrocities committed by the Bolsheviks during and after the Russian Revolution which led to the rise of communist expansionism, the Cold War, nuclear deterrence, and the absurdity of a policy of Mutually Assured Destruction (MAD), I was led to the further extremes suffered by the victims of China's fall into absolutism.

The vehemence and brutality of the communist takeover in China, followed by the crimes inflicted by the communists on those poor unfortunates living in the neighbouring countries such as Vietnam, Cambodia, North Korea and Tibet, both shocked and appalled me.

While writing this book, I thought that I could rather have been writing a fictionalised piece concentrating on characters that suffered horrendously at the hands of the communists to provide a more detailed description of their plight. I then realised that no fictional work could have the same impact as the true histories.

Instead, as with the first book in this series, I have written from a more optimistic viewpoint, attempting to show how such tragedies could have been averted and millions of lives saved, and also, I hope – showing how it would have been a much simpler task to achieve that victory over tyranny had we acted in the manner General Patton desired – *when* he wanted us to act.

To all of those who have served – those who have made sacrifices or given their lives to defend a liberated way of life – all of whom have fought to extend the virtues of individual liberty and democracy to other human beings, and to save those who could not defend themselves from tyranny – this book is for them.

THE FREE WORLD WAR II

A Probability of Evil

PROLOGUE

"The function of wisdom is to discriminate
between good and evil."
Marcus Tullius Cicero

Chinese Communist Party Headquarters,
Office of the Vice Chairman of the Military Commission
Yan´an, China
February 20th, 1947

A set of blackout curtains withdrew, sending bright light bursting into the room and revealing a brilliant clear sky over the surrounding snow-capped hills. Zhou Enlai blinked from the glare, and lamented yet another dry, chilly day in the northern Chinese city.

Zhou turned from the window at the sound of a polite knock, and a pair of tall wooden doors opened on the far side of the room. A man entered carrying a portfolio. The two bowed to each other, then their broad smiles cleared the formality from the air.

"Xiong!" said the Vice Chairman warmly. "Welcome back! I can tell this will be a glorious day for our cause!"

"One to light the path forward after the many years of darkness," replied Xiong.

"Yes, darkness ... but with all this freezing snow I'm almost looking forward to some rain and gloom" said Zhou, "At least it will be warmer."

Xiong moved to the conference table in the centre of the room. Buckles snapped as he opened his leather attaché case and withdrew the contents.

Zhou could barely repress a broad grin, and his eyes widened at what lay before them on the table.

Xiong unfolded one of the blueprints, "Moonflower has brought us the means of certain victory."

The Vice Chairman leaned forward and studied one of the plans intently, "Hmm, a 122mm gun; the KMT has nothing to withstand such a weapon."

"We will be receiving a prototype in a matter of days. It is on route from Kazakhstan."

"Only one tank? It is a shame it is not a whole company. There is word the Nationalists are closing in on us again."

The civil war was going badly for the communists. Chiang Kai-shek's government forces had been getting the better of the Chinese Red Army since hostilities had resumed following the end of the war in Europe. But the events of the previous days were going to turn the civil war in favour of the communists.

"And what of Moonflower?" asked Zhou.

"He will be with us shortly. He rises ... late," Xiong replied apologetically. He knew his prize's habits very well. As an intelligence agent it was his job to know. The homework he'd done had been instrumental in sequestering their man before Chiang's secret police had got to him.

As though reading the junior officer's mind, Zhou responded, "Your work will be well rewarded my young friend. The course of history changes with such twists."

His fingers shuffled through some of the other blueprints, bringing a wry smile to his distinguished features.

"We will get these plans to our factories in the northeast. It may take us many months, but our Peoples

Liberation Army will one day be the best equipped military force in Asia."

Xiong also flipped through more of the blueprints, then picked one out of the pile.

"Not just the army, Vice Chairman – look at this!"

Zhou's face lit up as he recognized the outlines of a type of engine he'd previously seen in roughly drawn sketches sent to him from his spies in Europe.

"A jet engine?"

"Correct ... and powering an aircraft so fast that ..."

A knock on the door interrupted the excitement.

The doors swung wide, and an aide entered, followed by a stocky Caucasian man with a crew-cut and thick moustache. His square-cut suit was a dull, plain grey and belied his imposing stature.

The foreigner held out his hand and Zhou accepted it, surprised by the soft skin and limp grasp.

The aide made the introductions. "Comrades ... please meet the petitioner for political asylum, the former Premier of the Soviet Union, Josef Vissarionovich Stalin."

Stalin's bow was a mere nod, a reluctant concession from a proud and once-powerful man who was now reduced to asylum-seeker. He looked at the design in Zhou's hands and with a tinge of arrogance, said, "Ah, I see you like the MiG that I have brought you."

CHAPTER ONE

A utopian free world looks back on its past.

The wars against Nazi Germany and Japan, and then communist Russia, have been won. The western Allies, together with General Andrey Vlasov's Russian Liberation Army, have overthrown the tyranny of Stalin's Bolshevism. Now Russia, with Vlasov as its new President, is becoming a benevolent democracy.

On the world stage, the original Charter of the United Nations, drafted in 1945, was seen to have been instigated under the corrupting influence of the Soviet Union. The United Nations was duly abolished, and a new global entity, The Union of Nations (UoN), was formed in its place.

The UoN's Charter was inspired by the recent triumphs of liberty over oppression, and of the individual over the state, and recognized that the basic human rights of every human being entitled them to liberty, democracy and equality. The Charter also sought to secure those rights by ensuring that all member governments derived their just powers from the consent of the governed, and that the people must possess the right, and democratic mechanism, to depose those in power when required.

One of the UoN's strictures was to ensure that only popular democracies held positions on the key councils, such as the Security Council. Any nations that failed to meet specific criteria, such as regularly scheduled elections, were excluded from full membership until the required statutory changes were implemented.

In the Far East, the communists under Mao Zedong finally prevailed in the civil war against the Nationalists of Chiang Kai-shek. They did not achieve this victory alone. Back in August 1945, the Soviets had invaded northern China and defeated the occupying Japanese Army in Manchuria. The Russian generals in command of those invading Soviet armies were mostly hardline communists and loyal to Stalin, and three thousand miles from Moscow in the Russian Far East, found themselves isolated from events when Vlasov's RLA had liberated the capital. With half a million men under their command and bolstered by many thousands of unrepentant communists escaping Moscow and arriving in the east, the Soviets resolved to hold out in Vladivostok, and even threatened to retake the capital.

And so began a covert alliance between communist China and the remaining Soviets. Assisted by Soviet military support and designs for their latest weaponry, the Chinese Communist Party (CCP) defeated the Kuomintang, or Nationalist Army in northern China, and then took over the entire country.

With another major communist threat emerging, the balance of power in the Asian region was shifting once more. Communist doctrine preached a class war, and that it was the duty of the proletariat to 'liberate' all others from the oppressive bourgeoisie. With the demise of communism in Moscow, China now saw itself as being alone in that struggle, and a deepening sense of paranoia infected the Party leadership. They quickly assigned all of their nation's resources to their military build-up, and with maniacal energy, brutally and barbarically imposed their ideology upon their own people. After the Chinese were subdued, the CCP made plans to extend the reach of communism throughout the Asia-pacific region.

Intelligence reports from the international community were presented to the Union of Nations and made them aware of the atrocities being committed by the CCP. The UoN decreed the communist state to be a threat to the stability of the region, and to world peace. Early in 1948, a resolution was proposed before the Security Council; to protect the lives and the human rights of the people of all countries at risk from the regime's aggression. If passed, the military resources and productive capacity of all member nations would be pledged to the support of military action, the intention of which would be to liberate those who had lost, or were in peril of losing, the rights assured them by the Charter of the UoN.

A further war to free the world from tyranny was now looming.

CHAPTER TWO

Dalnerechensk
250 miles north of Vladivostok
Far East Russia
May 25th, 1948

848th Motorised Rifle Battalion,
21st Russian National Guard Division
Russian Far East Front

Starshina Felix Mokady flicked off the safety catch on his PPSh-41 submachine gun. He checked his ammunition, *Only two more clips. Damn these shortages!* he thought angrily. *First the fuel for the tanks being rationed, and now we don't have enough bullets for our rifles.*

To his front, the light-brown dust cloud kicked up by the artillery barrage started to clear and he could once again see the dark-green cones of the treetops. His senses were slowly returning to normal, but all sounds of life from the taiga forest were now replaced by a penetrating silence.

Sleep ... then peace and quiet ... then morning barrage ... then attack. The same every day ... until we die.

The 21st Russian National Guard Division had been assaulting the Soviet-held town's outskirts for days. Those previous attacks had been failing as the men were already tired from fighting through miles of forest for weeks on end. That, together with a lack of tank support to break through the heavy defences around the town, was only causing the

Russian high command to push their infantry harder. The heavy losses were no problem, there were plenty of replacements, and there had even been rumours of them receiving armoured support. The Russian Airforce ruled the skies over the far east as the Soviets didn't have the resources to replace their losses, but planes and bombs alone could not win the war here.

The unit's lieutenant had been killed the previous day, so it was now up to Mokady. He stood out of his hole, raising his arm and checking to see if the eyes of his men were on their new leader.

A shuddering vibration rose from the ground beneath their feet. *Tanks!*

He looked around frantically, trying to determine the direction of their approach, then relaxed. *Oh spaseeba! Finally! They are ours!*

All around Mokady, heads were bobbing up, and more and more sets of eyes showed through dust-caked faces, looking to the starshina for the signal to move. He held his arm up, waiting for the lumbering T10's to pass through their lines so his men could form up behind them. As the nearest tank rumbled loudly past, the ground quaked and Mokady's hearing numbed again. He hardly noticed, as all thoughts of discomfort or self-preservation were brushed aside, and he felt the familiar rage rising up inside his beating chest.

Time to fight and kill once again.

He dropped his arm. Along with his own platoon, hundreds of infantrymen on either side swarmed out of their holes and followed the tanks. As Mokady trotted forward, his PPSh-41 cradled in his arms, he spotted an insignia on the T10's turret. The former symbol of the communist Red Army, a red star, had been painted over with that of the new

Russian Army – a white rectangle overlaid with a dark blue diagonal cross. As it always did, the sight of the flag brought back exultant memories of the battles he'd fought two years ago to free his homeland.

Back then, he'd been inspired by the same blue and white banner while serving under General Vlasov in the KONR – The Committee for the Liberation of the Peoples of Russia – the forerunner of the RLA. Now, many of those RLA soldiers were three thousand miles from Moscow, taking part in the spring offensive to clean out the last remnants of the same communist tyranny that had caused his country so much suffering.

Forty divisions of the new Russian Army had crossed the icy wastes of Siberia by rail and road during the previous winter, then waited months while their forces built up in Khabarovsk, four hundred miles from the enemy's coastal stronghold of Vladivostok.

Explosions burst among the trees ahead as the Red artillery fired blindly just in front of their own troops. Off to one side, a one-hundred-and-fifty-foot cedar received a direct hit, followed by a resounding crack as the tree snapped off from the two-metre wide trunk at its base. It crashed to the ground only yards in front of the T10 that Mokady's platoon was following. The tank braked and then swerved to go around the obstacle. The troops behind it broke formation to follow it, but several tried to continue straight on by clambering over the fallen trunk.

The starshina watched in horror as those men who were now exposed several feet above the ground, became prime targets for the enemy machine guns. Bodies jerked crazily as they were riddled with bullets, and blood and torn flesh flew from their broken bodies.

"Keep going! Stay behind the tanks!" Mokady shouted.

Other officers were yelling the same orders to their men. They needed to stay with the tanks to prevent the armour from becoming isolated and vulnerable to attack from the enemy's infantry anti-tank weapons.

"Move! Keep going!" he continued to shout even though his lungs and throat burned from the exertion. Through the trees he saw an T10 burst into flames, a victim of a Soviet SU-100 tank destroyer. Artillery continued to burst around the mass of advancing troops, and more enemy heavy machine-guns were opening up on them as they closed on the ruined buildings fringing the forest.

"Get to the tanks!" he cried, but his voice was weakening, and the men were faltering and going to ground.

Tired and hopeless eyes looked up at him. Men huddled and pressed themselves against the trees as bullets bit into the bark, and they desperately clutched their rifles to their chests like they were a shield against the death all around them.

Starshina Mokady couldn't blame them. They'd been fighting too far from home, and for too long without rest. That distance was also the cause of the painfully slow advance of the Russian Army toward their ultimate objective of Vladivostok. Supply lines were stretched too far and were resulting in shortages of fuel and ammunition.

Mokady, trying to rally his men, raised his PPSh-41 and fired a burst into the foliage ahead from which the enemy infantry were firing. It was a futile gesture. The Russian tanks continued to advance, unaware that the infantry that was supposed to be supporting them were flagging behind and would not be able to prevent attacks from enemy infantry. Inevitably, another T10 was blown up – its turret blown off sideways and away from the chassis. This one had been detonated by a satchel charge thrown onto the rear engine cover beside the turret ring. The Red Army soldier responsible hailed jubilantly to his comrades as he ran back to cover.

Infuriated, Mokady slammed his last clip into the receiver and fired a burst at the running tank-killer. At one hundred yards, none of his spraying bullets found their mark. He slumped behind a tree, watching with despair as the attack around him ground to a halt. Beside him on the ground lay a dead Soviet soldier. He picked up the submachine gun the dead man was still holding and looked at it. It was an exact copy of his own PPSh-41, but there were Chinese characters stamped on the metal plating.

As Mokady swapped the full magazine from the dead man's gun into his own, he realised why the Soviets were having no supply problems. He knew that his Russian Army would not be taking Dalnerechensk today, or be reaching Vladivostok by the end of summer. The Reds were better positioned and better supplied.

If President Vlasov's forces were going to liberate the last of their country's soil, they were going to need outside help.

As the survivors of the failed attack started retreating, Starshina Felix Mokady got up and joined them. He passed a T10 that had been abandoned because it had run out of fuel.

Boze moi! That sums it up, he thought with frustrated anger. *This whole debacle has run out of steam and we will spend another winter holed up on the edge of Siberia.*

As he dropped back into his weapon pit, he looked around for members of his depleted platoon. Half were still lying dead or wounded back among the trees.

I hope President Vlasov has some influence in the Union of Nations ... if we're going to defeat the communists we're going to need some friends.

CHAPTER THREE

"Who you were; who you are; who you will be."
Mantra of the Directory of Purpose

Mojave City
2268 CE

"Hesta, great news! We have some more work to do!" Arjon Aram announced to the bower.

"Online and awaiting input."

"Yes of course you are" he replied drily. "Two things, first we will need to establish a dedicated connection to the contributor network at the Directory of Purpose."

"Initiating. As they have a discriminatory endpoint there will be a delay before my request is white-listed."

"Right ... whatever that means. Secondly, we will be creating a series of matrices. In order for you to do that we will be receiving additional computational and storage resources, and increased bandwidth."

"What kind of matrices?"

Arjon was a little surprised at Hesta's question. Her requests for information were normally limited to trivia such as what he and Eya would like for dessert. When they were discussing his work, her heuristic programming usually prevented her from being too proactive so that she wouldn't be asking too many questions in advance while trying to meet some service-oriented goal.

"Hmm, we don't know exactly yet ... but the matrices will be extensions of the original we used for General

Patton's accident. As you're aware, that simulation has been uploaded to the DoP's internal systems."

"I see," said Hesta. "So, we will be expanding on that world to investigate further possibilities?"

"Correct"

"May I ask the nature of those enquiries?"

"Well ... that's a little premature at this stage ... but let me see ..."

Arjon couldn't help but feel that Hesta had received a recent upgrade without his knowledge.

It's possible he thought, *I know I sometimes skip over my messages, and I definitely listen to those mundane notifications she's always spouting as though we're in some kind of domestic relationship from previous centuries where men regularly tuned out from their spouses when they're talking. My gosh, I hope I'm not doing that with Eya?*

He quickly stifled his concern. He and Eya were so in love and spent so much time together either sating their desires or quelling them out of simple decency, that there was seldom a time they weren't completely in synch with each other.

He returned to pondering the human-machine interaction and how in the past there had been a level of static expectation, leading to a mindset of humans seeing their AIs at a new level. It was one that led to the question of whether they would eventually seek status as a sentient lifeform. *Ah, but the Enlightenment of the Soul has complicated that question ... and qwerty! I shudder at the thought of Hesta churning out machine-poetry!*

"Arjon?"

"Sorry Hesta, I got carried away with my train of thought ... what was the question again?" he asked, feeling sheepish at once again taking their domesticity for granted.

"The matrices, what will the theme of their inquiry be?"

"Hmm, well, it's not for my usual line of legal case-work but it will require my investigative skill set."

Since the Enlightenment of the Soul, Arjon had been working for several private clients, with cases stemming from the status of the new legal entity labelled the 'Human Spirit'. He had provided supporting evidence in one case where the plaintiff had sought compensation for the lost inheritance from their previous life.

The unclaimed estate had been appropriated by the state, but after the plaintiff proved the identity of their previous 'host', using a methodology similar to that used to find Buddhist incarnates, the proceedings established a number of legal precedents, including the process for confirming the identity of a former host-body.

"The Directory of Purpose has contacted me and is pursuing research related to the founding of our Pillars."

"Interesting" said Hesta.

"Yes ... very. I'm honoured that they have chosen me to assist them. We will be looking into the origins of the Pillars, with specific focus on the Spire of Evolution and the Bureau of Sanity."

"Why is the Directory interested in our past? Their Mission Statement focuses on what the human race needs to do in future so that humanity can achieve higher levels of evolution and understanding."

"Agreed ... and qwerty! The whole idea of that gets my head spinning! How are they going to do that? And what are they aiming for? Do they have something in mind – specific goals that give them some guidance? I expect that evolution will be pretty straightforward from a physical perspective, but what about understanding? Is that merely scientific or does it include the spiritual?"

"Arjon, please focus ... we'll be working on this together – I can provide you with a summary of the Directory's strategic plan and highlight the main points that will most likely affect your tasks."

"Good! Thank you." Arjon already felt his stress levels dropping, allowing him to speculate on the future. He imagined what it may be the Directory would be aiming at, some kind of garden utopia, more perfect than the world in which they now lived. In his mind, he saw himself with his loved one, Eya, in a state of perpetual bliss. It wouldn't matter to him what kind of habitat they lived in ... a shining crystal tower, an interstellar spacecraft, or a purpose-designed eternal garden – one which met all of their physical and spiritual needs. The important thing would be that they had attained the highest state of mind possible for an organic lifeform. They would be together ... perhaps immortal and travelling the stars for as long as the universe would allow.

The important thing for the DoP to begin with was what would be required to support all of the Arjons and Eyas? A civilisation based around automatons which would do all of the menial work? There might be consequences for such a dependence on machines. Perhaps a civilisation with a wholly organic culture – where life has evolved to provide everything that humans need without toil or suffering, including food and shelter if such concepts are still relevant. *Maybe we should aim at some kind of hybrid, where we are an impervious part of nature, but able to leave our doomed solar system in several million years to avoid its slow, inevitable death, and also find an independent way of perpetual living ... or somehow transfer our souls to a machine host – now there's a thought!*

"Arjon?"

Mmmm ... I'm thinking way too materially here ... what about the soul? What if we don't need to exist in this three-dimensional chaos anyway?

"Arjon!"

"Ahh ... apologies Hesta, I'm having a brainstorm." He stopped pacing and sat down into his oversized leather armchair. He felt himself comforted by the chair's embrace as it had thousands of times before. Its internal mechanisms moulded its cushioning around him, instilling a feeling of buoyancy. His overactive mind slowed to a more reasonable tempo. *Ahhh ... perhaps everyone should simply live in one of these chairs.*

One concept presented itself – wherever they lived, it was the people's state of mind, their self-esteem and self-actualization, that mattered the most. If they were part of a society which exuded goodwill and ethically-driven happiness, one where no-one covets that which another possesses – then their world would shape itself around them. The Directory would need to focus on helping people achieve a perfect state of mind.

"Hesta!" He rose from his chair and once again began to pace slowly around the den, "We will be using a simulation to research the past – the origins of the Spire of Evolution and the Bureau of Sanity ... so we can derive a baseline."

"A baseline?"

"Yes. From that simulation, I believe the Directory may be able to glean the requirements for a model for the ideal human condition."

A silence permeated the den for several seconds. Arjon could sense that Hesta's vast computational resources were processing a response.

"How will they manifest such a model?" she asked.

"Ha! That will be something to see!" he exclaimed as he went to the window. Outside, a lush greenscape stretched to the horizon. One of rolling grasslands dotted by patches of forest and broken not by fences, but by gentle watercourses. It was a land that had once been an inhospitable desert. *Just as the recent Enlightenment has shown us,* he thought solemnly, *we'd been living in a spiritual desert ... unaware of our souls and believing our minds had already attained an ultimate state. Maybe now, we should try to find out how to get to that perfect garden, or spaceship...or wherever it is that people want to be.* He relished the view outside. *If we can change a wasteland for the better, then why not ourselves?*

He turned from the window and mused out loud, "Perhaps we need to simulate a perfect man and woman – so that we can have an example for the rest of us?"

CHAPTER FOUR

*"The duty of and ultimate goal of every communist is to
overthrow the bourgeoise and to create
an international republic."*
Excerpt from Chinese Communist Doctrine

Headquarters Supreme Commander Allied Powers (SCAP)
Tokyo
Sept. 15th, 1948
1100 HRS

The view from the 5th floor of the Dai-ichi building
showed a city slowly emerging from its ruins. Two-thirds of
Tokyo had been destroyed by fire during the Pacific War. Its
people were now rebuilding both their homes and their culture.

As he gazed out of the window, Major General Charles
Willoughby pondered the remainder of his day. As the head
of the military intelligence section, or G2, of General Douglas MacArthur's far-eastern command, SCAP, his calendar
was full of planning sessions with his staff. Most of those
would be dealing with the occupation force's clean-up of the
cartels and Japanese military-industrial conglomerates, or
zaibatsu. He turned to his desk and leafed through his diary.
The next meeting scheduled in a few minutes time was described by just three letters ... CIG.

*Hmmm ... Central Intelligence Group...used to be the
OSS. Name makes them sound even spookier than before.*

Taking a seat in his padded leather chair, he was about to press the intercom to call his aides-de-camp when it buzzed at him, and a voice announced that the meeting attendee had arrived.

"Send him in" he said as he stood up and started to the door. When it opened, a tall officer wearing the uniform of a US Army Colonel walked in.

"Nice to finally meet you in person Colonel Blackett" said Willoughby as they shook hands.

"Likewise, General" replied Blackett.

The two sat down opposite each other at the desk and Willoughby smoothed his dark hair as he read through a thick report that had been provided to him for the meeting. The General's manner reminded Blackett of a fox. Willoughby exhumed an intellectual air, while effortlessly analysing the world around him.

Blackett opened his attaché case and took out a notebook, "I see you received the briefing notes I forwarded to your office" he said.

"I'm afraid I haven't had time to do more than skip through its contents" Willoughby said a little impatiently.

The CIG Colonel wasn't surprised. He was used to the higher-up officers always being short of time, but he frowned slightly to reveal his disappointment.

"Well then", said Blackett, "let me provide the necessary background. You would of course be aware of our activities in the Russian Far East and Manchuria for the past eighteen months," he stated.

"Only that your CIG has been active there – no details from Washington ... need to know basis only, as you would know."

"Yes, of course. Well, we've been conducting surveillance operations with the intention of confirming the production of armaments by the Chinese – the designs for which were provided to them by the Soviets."

Willoughby barely nodded, still reading through his own set of notes, then asked a question that Blackett was expecting. "Do we know exactly *who* it was that provided those designs?"

"Who? Does it matter? We've been working under the assumption it was someone high up in the former Soviet regime in Moscow."

Willoughby sighed. It seemed he was disappointed with Blackett's response. "High up yes ... but how high up do you think? As high as Stalin himself?"

Blackett eyed the intelligence chief warily, sensing he was being probed for something he personally didn't know, but Willoughby had suspicions about. "Stalin? But he was killed in a plane crash ... wasn't he?"

Willoughby grinned cagily, "That's the accepted story ... yes. But what do you, or your CIG *really* think?"

Blackett smiled back. He'd heard rumours from within the CIG about an unidentified codename showing up in intelligence reports – 'Moonflower'. The reports were related to the possibility that Stalin was still alive, but Blackett wasn't the kind of operative to work under such an assumption until there was something more than speculation to go on. "I can't speak for the CIG ... but personally I wouldn't discount the possibility he staged his own death and then somehow made it to China. He was, or still is, a very devious son of a bitch."

Willoughby nodded thoughtfully, and then returned to his reading.

Blackett picked up his own copy of the report and lay it on top of the notebook in his lap, "You'll notice on page 25 of the report there's a list of the suspected blueprints the Soviets provided to the Chinese."

Willoughby leafed through to the relevant page and then his eyebrows raised as he flipped over several pages of ordinance, including infantry weapons, armour, artillery and aircraft.

Blackett continued, "An operation is currently in progress to ascertain which of these weapons are still under development, and which are in full production. Much of the infrastructure for producing them has been in place in Manchuria for some years, courtesy of the Japanese occupation. The Soviets we know, have been helping the Chinese make modifications to the factories and machinery in the region – we expect it is for the purposes of widespread production of arms from those blueprints."

"And no doubt they plan to build other facilities in the south" added Willoughby gravely. "How long do we think this has been occurring?"

"Our information has been inconsistent," answered the Colonel with some hesitation, "You must understand that the fervour with which the communists are purging any opposition to their regime is making our job very difficult."

Blackett grimaced as he explained further, "While I was in China attached to the Kuomintang Nationalists as a military advisor last year, I saw what the communists were doing to the people who didn't think the same way as they did."

The recollections were clearly painful as he dug them out of some deep corner of his memory. "Arrests, beatings, torture ... and killings – we found some very gruesome evidence left behind after the Nationalists overtook territory previously under communist control."

"Oh? As bad as the Nazis – or the Bolsheviks?" asked Willoughby.

"Far worse sir" Blackett replied heavily. "It's like the Chinese are naturally inclined to commit atrocities in the name of whatever power they are being subjected to ... the Emperor, the warlord – or the Party."

Blackett shifted in his chair, fixing his eyes on Willoughby as though he needed to connect with the General and make him understand the magnitude of what he'd personally witnessed. Something so heinous and barbaric, but he only had a few sentences in which to do it.

"They destroy the lives of their own people ... make them 'confess' in self-criticism sessions, where every thought they have is exposed to the entire village. They make them accuse and betray their family and neighbours in front of the other villagers. There is no other outcome other than the guilty being sentenced to death ... and then the villagers are forced to take part in the executions – which are usually implemented by beating them to death. The process is Mao's way of ensuring that every single communist takes responsibility for their revolution."

He sighed, "They have destroyed the individual – the human spirit – leaving only drones ... slaves to the will of the Party."

Willoughby could sense Blackett's angst, and shared his outrage at the atrocities to which the other had been privy. Blackett took a sip of water. His eyes closed for a moment. The weight of his first-hand knowledge of the communist insanity required him to isolate those memories back to the remote corners of his mind; somewhere they couldn't impair or offend his sense of personal liberty and freedom.

"So" he added after a few moments, "... accurate intel of their preparations for war have been difficult to get hold of. Not just because of the extreme risk to informants, but also due to the highly effective methods being used to indoctrinate and brainwash the entire population. Reliable and verified information is very hard to obtain without us putting our agents in harm's way. One thing we do know however, is that communist doctrine preaches the spread of communism ... to all countries of the world."

Willoughby drank from his own glass of water, thinking for some time before closing the meeting. "This is too serious a problem for my office to deal with effectively" he said plainly. "We have our hands full with weeding out the last remnants of the old Bushido culture here in Japan." He swung his chair around to face the window. The sun was now at its zenith, bathing Tokyo in the warm glow of renewed hope that had been growing since the end of the war in the Pacific. *The Japanese are clawing their way out of the shadows*, he thought, but as he looked through the tinted glass in the direction of China on the other side of the Sea of Japan, he saw another country clouded beneath a looming shadow, and his perspective was darkened by another impending war.

China, Russia and the Korean peninsula were all within several hundred miles. The inhabitants of the shattered city below him could not face being part of another conflict, but Willoughby was sure that Japan would be central to the strategies of both sides. He turned back to Blackett, "General MacArthur will need to be appraised of any developments as soon as you can provide them to me."

Blackett gave Willoughby a look of concern, "General, I've been hearing from an associate of mine who is in Manchuria, just how serious these developments are. I'll be meeting him in Tibet in a few weeks to retrieve his report on the Chinese build-up in Manchuria. He has also informed me of Chinese intentions in Korea, a country where he's previously taken part in operations to recruit agents from within the North Korean military.

"Well Colonel, those *are* operations I've been briefed on by Washington, and this office will be looking to exploit those assets at the appropriate time."

"I see, but with the situation building in China as it is, I hope consideration is being given to ways we might move events along more...*urgently?*"

Willoughby appreciated the other's candour, and with a few minutes left before his next meeting, he asked the CIG officer to expand on his statement, "Tell me Colonel, how do you suggest we *move events along?*

"General ... I believe we need to find ourselves another Vlasov."

Willoughby smiled shrewdly, "It's interesting you should say that Colonel ... because I think we may have already found one."

CHAPTER FIVE

Baotou Armaments Factory
Inner Mongolia
Sept. 19th, 1948

Valentin Rhuzkoi adjusted his tunic, giving it a firm shrug downwards with both hands. It was the uniform of a full colonel in the 1st Far Eastern Front of the renegade Soviet Army, one level higher than his real rank of Lieutenant Colonel in Vlasov's Russian Army.

Beside him, P'eng Xi followed his lead and brushed off some of the dust on his sleeve that had been picked up while walking from their car. He wore the uniform of a Shao Wei, or 2nd lieutenant, in the Manchurian Field Army. It was a rank he'd achieved after years of fighting in the Chinese civil war, but not with the communists. The current need for officers to enforce collectivisation in China had led the CCP to recruit from the vanquished Nationalists. P'eng had taken the opportunity to return to military service, not only for the material benefits, but also as a way of restoring his service to the cause of liberty he believed in – as a spy.

He nodded affirmatively at Rhuzkoi, confirming that they both looked the part. A man entered the foyer, bowed briefly and announced in faltering Russian, "Welcome to Factory 647, Manager Ching-zao will see you."

Rhuzkoi put the man at ease by acknowledging that he spoke Mandarin, which caused the official to smile with relief. The two officers followed him down a corridor to a reception room. Tables lined one wall, replete with dishes of hors d'oeurve. The centrepiece was a large dish of black caviar topped by a miniature flag displaying a hammer and sickle on a red background. There were other offerings to honour their Soviet guest, including Pelmeni dumplings and vodka. On the wall above the tables, portraits of Mao, Stalin and Lenin looked down upon the banquet.

"Please help yourselves while we wait for Manager Ching-zao," said the man, who promptly bowed and left. P'eng's eyes widened at the elaborate spread containing delicacies he had not seen in years.

"I can't believe it," he said.

"Da, I expect this is not from the factory cafeteria," said Rhuzkoi.

P'eng looked at the spread guiltily, knowing how the workers out on the factory floor would be living on meagre rations, but the two started eating anyway – they had to play their roles as accurately as possible.

The official returned with several other guests and made the introductions. Most were senior management, but a few were local Party representatives, assigned to the factory to 'inspire' the workers.

"Ah, you are enjoying the caviar we obtained for you Colonel!" Manager Ching-zao boasted as he entered through the main doors. The manager and his guests bowed.

"I am humbled by your gracious welcome Manager" said Rhuzkoi.

Although not obese, Ching-zao was obviously very well fed, and he filled a plate while talking, "We endeavour to share the rewards of our dedicated service to the Party" he said roundly. "Now, eat up! We have much to show you!"

After lunch, the group left the reception and began a tour of the facility.

"We have expanded the number of production lines for all models of armoured vehicles from twelve up to twenty in just the past year!" Ching-zao claimed with pride as the group walked across a compound filled with piles of steel sheeting and hoppers filled with raw materials. A line of smokestacks edged the open space between buildings, and workers hurried around urgently while they were in view of the management.

"We will avoid the foundry area" said the Manager, "It gets uncomfortably hot in there, so we will start at the milling plant."

"How many acres does the facility cover?" asked Rhuzkoi.

"Ha! Acres ... you should be asking me how many square miles!"

The stocky Manager swept his arm over the enormous site, "Over six square miles, including two power plants, a rail terminal and over eighty thousand workers!"

Rhuzkoi could believe it. He knew how cruelly efficient the communists were at applying the vast human resources at their disposal. *Just like building the pyramids,* he thought with some sadness, *though less use of the whip and more use of psychological coercion.* He forced himself to keep his temper in check, and his patience. He wasn't here to be impressed by the scale of the CCP's military production, he needed to see what they were producing. It was another hour before they were shown what he'd come to see.

Inside a large brick building, the final assembly plant which housed one of the production lines, they saw the outcome of all of the raw materials, iron smelting and parts fabrication. It was where the results of the blueprints provided to the CCP by Stalin two years earlier were now coming to fruition.

"Comrades! This is the most powerful armoured vehicle in the world!" Ching-zao exclaimed proudly. "It has been designated the WZ-10 by our glorious leader Mao Zedong." The Chinese guests were clapping emphatically as Ching-zao patted the barrel of the 120mm gun.

Rhuzkoi was amazed that the top of the low-profile tank's turret was only seven feet from the ground, making it a very difficult target to hit in the right terrain.

"Production output has now reached a total of 20 units per week from the four dedicated production lines" added Ching-zao.

"How much of an increase is that over previous months?" asked Rhuzkoi, feigning mild interest while he was mentally compiling the numbers to deduce a total production output.

"Mmm ... it has been varied. Early on we had many supply problems which we have addressed over time" The manager laughed, "I see our Soviet comrades need to know how many of these beasts we have hidden away from prying eyes!" The Manager nodded to an assistant who gave Rhuzkoi a printed copy of an inventory.

"Please enjoy this reading to assist you with your report on our progress here! It is a full report of our production of all models of armoured vehicles produced here since our foundation. Meanwhile I will inform our other guests of some details that you may already know, since the design of this particular tank was intended to become the IS10?"

Rhuzkoi merely smiled, not wanting to give away anything that might later compromise his impersonation.

The Manager then continued as he ran his hand over the freshly painted dull green frontal armour, "Over ten inches thick so it is impenetrable to any of the guns of the western imperialist tanks!"

After a few more minutes speaking to the others, Ching-zao then took Rhuzkoi aside, "Of course Colonel, we have your Prime Minister Stalin to thank for this design" he said humbly, "... and the tank's designation of WZ10 is derived from 'IS10' – and is in his honour."

Rhuzkoi was taken aback. The Manager was clearly speaking of Stalin in the present tense – as though he were alive. And he called him Prime Minister, whereas Stalin was the Premier of the Soviet Union at the time of his death. Rhuzkoi suddenly realised that he could be on the verge of uncovering an extremely well-kept secret. He collected his thoughts, and then responded vaguely, "You're very gracious Manager ... I'm certain that the ... eh ... Prime Minister ... would wish to be here to witness the result of his efforts – to see the communist ideology spread throughout the world, and also to one day see the communist party restored in our own homeland."

Ching-zao frowned as though wounded, "A great pity he is currently so inconvenienced. I'm certain that with our help both he and you will get to see such a day arrive."

Rhuzkoi had a flash of inspiration, "So tell me Manager, when was the last time you saw Prime Minister Stalin?"

"Why ... I thought you would have been aware of his secret visit to this factory when we first began production? Let me see, it was over a year ago ... I have been sworn to secrecy, but I can find out the exact date if you like?"

"No, no that will not be necessary ... I was just curious – it will assist to put the findings of my own report in perspective – thank you."

Rhuzkoi began to feel uncomfortable with the direction in which the conversation could be heading. He didn't want the Manager to start asking questions about Stalin's current whereabouts which he would not be able to answer. He preempted his host, "As you know, we patriotic defenders of the 1st Soviet Far Eastern Front under Marshal Meretskov are committed to the return of our Prime Minister to his rightful post in Moscow...and we will ensure those reactionary puppets serving Vlasov will be sent to the gallows."

Ching-zao puffed out his chest, "The Chinese Communist Party will be there at your side!", then half-bowed and enquired deviously, "Tell me ... just how strong *is* the Soviet position around Vladivostok?"

Rhuzkoi had to be careful. He hadn't been to the isolated port city and final outpost of Russian communism for over a year.

"Morale is high ... but we could not hold out so long as we have done without the material support of your country. We have desperate need of continued supplies and weapons – such as this this new tank."

"And you shall have them! We too are glad we are not alone; and we will spread our glorious revolution – not just back to your own unfortunate country, but to all of our less privileged neighbours who are being subverted by the imperialist west."

Rhuzkoi rejoined P'eng and they completed their tour before leaving the factory complex with the information handed to them by the factory management. It also contained detailed specifications for the other armoured vehicles produced at the huge plant, including the WZ-54 medium tank which had been under development in the former Soviet Union as the T-54.

Rhuzkoi decided to keep the revelation regarding Stalin still being alive to himself for now. He would only be passing this new information on to Colonel Blackett in their next contact.

"The production in this facility and others around the country, far exceeds that needed for maintaining a defensive posture," he told P'eng.

"I believe you are correct" replied the Chinese officer. "After the Russian communists were thrown out of Moscow there has been an increased sense of isolation in this country," he warned. "It is as though the Party has become more paranoid and fearful than before. They are no longer just crushing the spirit of our people but are now also directing that aggression outwards at the rest of the world."

Rhuzkoi sighed, "Yes I have seen this before in Russia," he said, remembering a similar mentality that had affected the Bolsheviks and driven them to acts of social genocide in their own and neighbouring countries. "But the Chinese communists will soon be completely alone with their ideology, and will no doubt be more aggressive in their efforts to sustain it."

The Russian thought grimly, *Another war against tyranny on the horizon. I hope the rest of the world has the stomach for it.*

CHAPTER SIX

Chamdo,
North-eastern Tibet
Sept. 30th, 1948

At the roof of the world, a pristine blue sky touched the white tops of the mountains, and the cold dry air foretold the coming of winter. A flight of bar-headed geese climbed upwards, continuing their passage over the Himalayas on the highest altitude migration on the planet.

The Mekong River, swollen by recent rains, tumbled its way over ancient boulders and past the town of Chamdo. Its epic journey would take it out of the Himalayas, and down to Vietnam on its way to the South China Sea.

Colonel William Blackett squinted against the bright daylight as he took stock of the magnificent surroundings. The autumn leaf fall in the mountains had finished early, leaving the towering wall of slopes covered in patches of bare trees between the evergreen pines. Above them, the exposed brown slopes above the treeline led up to snow-capped peaks. He breathed deeply, relishing the thin air, but it increased the feeling of light-headedness caused by the altitude. His skin was tanned from exposure to the harsher sun at this higher elevation, and his dark hair was freshly crew cut courtesy of the barber at the nearby Tibetan Army post.

As he stood on the dirt porch at the front of a small but neat house within earshot of the gently flowing Mekong, the front door opened behind him and a uniformed man brought out a tray of tea.

"Good morning Colonel. I trust you slept well?" asked Phuntsok Chozom, a Lieutenant in the Tibetan Army.

"Yes, extremely well," replied Blackett. "This cool climate and the tranquillity are doing me a world of good ... my sleep included."

Sleep was a precious commodity for him, especially under circumstances where one's peace of mind could be shattered at any time by the onset of an impending conflict on this remote frontier. The Chinese Army were on their way, moving thousands of troops up to the nearby border. There was no doubt in Blackett's mind that the peaceful land of Tibet was on China's list of neighbouring countries to be consumed in the name of communist expansion.

"Tell me," asked Blackett, "... does the Mekong ever flood here?"

Phuntsok handed the Colonel a cup of steaming chai, and with a thoughtful frown answered, "We call the river 'Dzuchu'. It will only flood if there has been a landslide downstream, and the waters become backed up."

Blackett looked some distance downstream, to the where the river left the town and passed between the two steep grey rock vertices of a ravine. He imagined the thousands of miles that the water had to travel before it reached the coast and wondered at the millions of lives it touched on its way.

This thin air really is getting to me, he thought as a childish impulse to put a toy boat in the water and see how far it floated downstream crossed his mind.

He glanced at his watch, *Rhuzkoi's late. Hope he hasn't had any trouble getting here.*

There were very few good roads in Tibet, and to travel by horseback from Lhasa to this very remote outpost would have taken weeks. The CIG field team in Chamdo, himself and a radio operator, had parachuted in the previous week.

They'd brought their radio and a supply drop of arms for the Tibetans. Lt. Colonel Rhuzkoi was to join them by the same method of insertion this morning after an extended flight by long-range bomber from the Russian far east. Phuntsok was having coincident thoughts, "I expect our guest will be here shortly."

Blackett nodded and drank some tea. The village hugging the slopes around them was coming to life. Prayer flags fluttered in the morning breeze and a few white clouds started forming above the mountains. The sound of bells clamoured as they swung lazily from the necks of a group of yaks being herded up to graze for the day in a highland meadow. Isolated for millennia, Tibet was a country like no other. The way of life of even the wildest nomads, the Khampa horsemen, was imbued with deep spiritual connections to the land itself, to Buddhism and its philosophy of compassion, and to the Dalai Llama.

To westerners such as Blackett, the Tibetans seemed almost child-like in their simplicity and trusting natures. Theirs was a culture which was more than just spiritual – it manifested the faith they had in the afterlife, in their daily interactions with the spirits of their ancestors – and in the significance of all living things.

Central to their beliefs was reincarnation, the transcendence of the soul to other levels of existence. This instilled within them a deep respect for life and all things living. It generated a harmonic balance between humans and their Earth which very few human civilisations had attained.

Blackett, sitting with his back leaning against the solid stone of the house, felt a warmth seeping into his bones. Not just from the heat of the sun soaking into the bricks, but a tangible comfort at being among a people with a wholly beneficent lifestyle. It was a drastic contrast to the years of war in his past he'd rather forget. He closed his eyes for a moment, listening to the gentle sounds of harmony around him. When he opened them again, Lt. Colonel Rhuzkoi was walking up the path.

CHAPTER SEVEN

"I wish to be of the faction that desires to avoid the oppression of the poor people of this miserable nation upon whom one cannot look without a bleeding heart."

Oliver Cromwell
25th April 1646

NK 105th Armoured Brigade
Maehyeon-ri,
North Korea
March 15th, 1949

General Yong-nam Choe strolled along the boardwalk overlooking the Imjin River and peered through the forest of barbed wire barring him from the riverbank below. The greenish-brown waters flowed energetically, carrying spring meltwater toward the western coast.

Yong-nam had walked along this tree-lined bank of the river carrying a fishing pole as a boy, but it had looked and felt very different then. There had only been one Korea. Along this river which now formed part of the border between north and south, there had been a single overgrown path leading to an occasional large rock where one could sit and throw in a line. Now, that same river was flanked by a mass of concrete bunkers, trenches and minefields.

In his boyhood he'd day-dreamed of the spirits inhabiting this place, the ones from the tales his father had told him. Stories of great water-snakes hunting in the eddies, and of benevolent dragons watching him from their eyries in the heights above the river.

He paused at a sand-bagged lookout post manned by two of his lower ranks. The men snapped to attention and saluted the General. Yong-nam nodded an acknowledgement and told them to carry on. As he raised his field-glasses and scanned the opposite bank for signs of enemy activity, he thought of the massive troop movements going on behind his own lines. His North Korean 105th Armoured Brigade was almost at full strength, and he smiled ruefully at the firepower building up under his command. Two full battalions of armour, one comprised of WZ-54 medium tanks based on the Soviet T54 design, and the other a mixed battalion of 155mm tank destroyers and SP guns. The tank destroyers were Chinese built, whose development had been based on the Soviet Obj 268.

All were crewed by North Koreans, who had been trained by the Chinese. In the next few days he would be receiving the last of his artillery and some older Russian SP guns. The latter worried him, as they were to be crewed by units drawn from the Soviets still holding out around Vladivostok. He knew those Soviet armies were under great pressure from President Vlasov's Russian armies, so wondered how they could spare the SP's? The only answer he could think of was that the Soviets were also being rearmed and reinforced by the Chinese.

A movement on the far riverbank caused Yong-nam to reflexively adjust focus and zoom in. It was an ROK soldier filling his canteen. Two other sentries joined him, and then they resumed their routine pass along the tree-lined stretch of river. As usual, there was no sign of the Republic of Korea shoring up their defences here. No outward sign that they knew of the tens of thousands of North Korean troops arriving at the border region by road and rail.

General Yong-nam put down his glasses and resumed his walk. The irony of the situation struck him. He knew that the massive build-up of communist forces at the border was merely a defensive measure, a response by the paranoid CCP at being the last bastion of extreme socialism on the planet. Ironic, because he had been feeding that paranoia by providing false reports of an equally massive build-up by the ROK Army on the southern side of the river. The next reconnaissance report from his brigade, verified by several of his most trusted officers, would not describe a few South Koreans on sentry duty, but sightings of armour and increased troop movements.

He thought of the words that the Russian agent, Rhuzkoi had said to him while he was being recruited by the west the previous year. *We need you to move things along here and make sure it looks as though the communists are starting a war.*

He wasn't sure why, but the Russian had also compared his intended role to that which Andrey Vlasov had played early on in the war against Stalin.

The spring air, the gentle murmur of the river ... it was the same peaceful setting in which he'd spent many hours as the boy with a vivid imagination.

Knowing it was a peace that would soon be shattered, he made a conscious effort to relish it while it lasted. He felt light-hearted as he relived some of those times, and looked up, searching the surrounding cliffs for anything unusual. The nest of a large bird, some broken branches in the trees, or any other sign of the dragons his father had told him about. The dragons who would be watching when the humans began to kill each other again. The killing in a war that he was to ensure would soon begin.

CHAPTER EIGHT

Mojave City
2268 CE

"Sweetheart ... will you read to me?" asked Eya.
"Look in thy glass and tell the face thou viewest,
Now is the time that face should form another,
Whose fresh repair if now thou not renewest,
Thou dost beguile the world, unbless some mother.
Thou art thy mother's glass, and she in thee
Calls back the lovely April of her prime."
"*Ooh!* Such a beautiful sonnet! You always find some-
thing so wonderfully flattering!" she said.
"It's inevitable when it's for you my treasure," explained
Arjon, "although it's only an excerpt from Shakespeare's
original. I just recalled that which I felt was most appropriate for you."
"How thoughtful ... but my love, would you still love me
if I changed?" she asked. "If one day I grew tired of looking
in the mirror and decided that my face should form another?"
"I love you for who you are" he admitted to her. Then,
taking her in his arms he expounded passionately, "But you
are breathtaking! I will have failed in my attentions if you
ever feel you are anything less than perfect!"
Arjon lay her down on a bed of silk-moss, "I can barely
contain the passion my heart seeks to unleash!"
Eya giggled, "Then let loose your passion! Your exotic
goddess ... your flaming-maned temptress awaits!"

The two lovers gave themselves to each other completely beneath a sheet of fragrant rose petals. The flora in the bower's garden around them seemed to shimmer with a shared delight at their coupling.

Later on, as he lay next to her, Arjon gazed dreamily across the smooth curve of Eya's midriff and into the garden. His thoughts were enamoured by their recent lovemaking, bringing on a rare compulsion to wax poetic. He resisted quoting any poetry, but pronounced his feelings to his lover. "When I make love to you it's like I'm the first man on Mars...marvelling in breathless wonder at a never-before visited dreamscape."

She kissed him passionately, then looked at him with a mischievous glint in her eye, "Well now you've conquered Mars...won't you want to explore somewhere else?"

He smiled innocently, "If you've found Heaven then why would you want to go downhill from there?"

Eya giggled and then got up to wander around. She tended the flowering plants diligently, so that the delphiniums, frangipani and red roses which were all in bloom, filled the bower with their scent.

"You've outdone yourself this year," said Arjon, admiring a jasmine vine in flower as it looped itself up into the lower branches of a magnolia tree.

"It *is* inspiring isn't it? I think my artwork benefits from the time I spend here."

Eya leant down and cupped her hand, lifting it up brimming with petals. When she was a girl, she'd fantasised of sleeping beneath a rose bed, with the velvety carpet of petals cushioning her dreams. She felt a warmth at the memory and savoured the innocence that her childhood dreams could retain.

She turned to Arjon, seeing him as a perfect complement to those dreams. She knew that the place they held in each other's hearts was a sanctuary from any disruption the world outside could muster.

Eya returned to the bed of silk moss and knelt beside Arjon. She let the petals in her hand cascade down onto his chest and added absently, "I'm getting a reputation among our friends as a horticulturist. They're always asking me for advice they can't always seem to find in an AI's searches."

"It's your personal touch," said Arjon, picking up a petal and tasting it. "I sometimes get that for my legal knowledge even though the information is readily available from an AI. Some things still get lost in translation when humans and machines communicate."

"Well I may have to get more impersonal and business-like in future, I've been recommended to the Spire of Evolution to take part in a research project."

"Really? That's impressive! What kind of research?" he asked.

"There's been little detail as yet, but I do know that it has some relevance to the human relationship with the natural world."

She nudged him gently, "So if I'm accepted there may be two of us being held in high esteem ... with inflated egos to match. Think there'll still be room in here for both of our giant heads?"

Arjon laughed. Since his involvement with the revelations surrounding General Patton, his reputation and social profile had skyrocketed. He'd been careful not to let it go to his head, and frequently checked the urge to discuss the topic at dinner parties, unless Eya tactfully brought it up. He preferred to keep his relationship with his friends the way it always had been.

"If you keep feeding my ego as well as you've been feeding these plants, I doubt there will be room."

Hours later, Arjon entered his den, "Hesta, please prepare to accept these parameters for the matrix beginning in 1948."

"Ready to instantiate declarations."

"First, a little background to assist you to frame your inputs. It seems the establishment of both the Spire of Evolution and the Bureau of Sanity were significantly influenced by the philosopher Ji-zhu Geist. Some details are known of his activity in Tibet during the war there, but little is recorded in our own history of his early years. We will examine an extension of the simulation in which General Patton was prematurely killed so we can compare those events to the corresponding period in our own incomplete history."

While Arjon paced around and explained, Hesta's heuristic programming allowed her to interpret the essence of his statements and convert them to a programmatic form, or machine code, which could then be processed by the matrix's artificial reality engine.

Arjon continued to describe the preliminary stage of his research for the Directory of Purpose, "This comparison will allow us to do two things. First, reconstruct Ji-zhu's past and determine the influence he had in that alternate world. Second, we will use that reconstruction to assist us with confirming what happened in his early years within our own history."

"I see. Will that process be an acceptable methodology for the Directory?"

"I would not expect that it would meet the criteria required by the Centre of Truth ... but it will be sufficient to support the further work by the Directory in this project. If we build a circumstantial retrospective, then we can provide some clarity around Ji-zhu's contribution to the formation of two of the Pillars, using er, let me see, um ... human analysis."

He wasn't sure if that last part would offend Hesta in any way, and he waited tentatively for a response. Silence ensued, so he stopped pacing around and flopped into his big leather chair. "Alright, let's start with the invasion of Tibet by the Chinese communists. Focus on the events immediately prior to the military incursion into eastern Tibet in October 1950."

The difference in dates between the simulation and his own history needed to be clarified, "Just to be certain of that date – that's October 1950 in the simulation – not the date of the Chinese invasion in our own history which occurred in March 1949. The discrepancy is due to the influence of the collapse of the Soviet bloc in 1946 which of course did not occur in the simulation."

"Date parameters confirmed."

Arjon had done extensive pre-reading about the Himalayan country and its people for this project. Tibet, a land of extreme climate due to its high altitude, where due to its harsh and inhospitable environment, every grain of barley, blackberry or drop of yak's milk was received with reverent gratitude. Rather than this harshness and austerity leading to a culture of barbarous materialism and greed for the scant resources, it had led to a unique brand of spiritualism. Most Tibetans sought to revere all living creatures – to value them and respect them, in the same manner as they expressed their compassion toward all other people who were living, or who had passed.

"Following that, we will concentrate on the role of the United Nations in that simulation and compare it to the actions taken by our own Union of Nations."

"All parameters initialized – inputting and compiling."

"Good. That should be enough for now. There are sure to be some contingent factors to be applied once the matrix is built."

"I'll notify you when it is complete," said Hesta.

CHAPTER NINE

NK 105th Armoured Brigade HQ
Maehyeon-ri,
North Korea
Sunday March 27th, 1949
0430 HRS

Major Ban Kyung slowed his staff car as it entered the transport park, careful not to disturb the canvas rucksack of goods he'd filled at the local market the previous evening. Regardless of his efforts, the wine bottles rattled as he applied the parking brake and the car stuttered to a halt. Kyung looked over his shoulder anxiously and checked that his hoard was still intact; rice wine, candies, sweet rice cakes and honey pastries, as well as a supply of his favourite gochujang red pepper sauce.

Usually he'd just stash a few treats in his pack if he was going on exercise. An impending war was a different story. *If there's going to be a full-scale conflict no sense in suffering through it without a decent supply of comforts,* he thought.

When he'd left the brigade HQ command post in the early hours to go on his shopping trip, the usual sluggish night-time routine had been going on around camp. The HQ tank company undergoing maintenance checks under lights, guards changing watch, and a few troops being drilled. Now, as he walked toward the CP entrance, he noticed the men around him moving with a sense of urgency. Dispatch riders were hurrying in and out of the sandbagged entrance, carrying orders, and he heard the sound of tank engines being warmed up from among the trees nearby. A flight of Mig 15 jets flown by the Chinese air force passed overhead.

He went straight to General Yong-nam's office, and was joined along the way by Captain Yee, the Operations officer. The two junior officers saluted the General smartly, and Yong-nam glared at Kyung to let him know he wasn't impressed that his adjutant had not been on hand during the preceding hour.

The General looked at the Operations officer, "Captain, I want you to contact each of our regiment's headquarters personally and ensure they are on standby."

"Yes General!"

Yong-nam stepped back behind his desk and carefully checked a note on the table, "We are expecting the order to come through anytime now … the code will be 'Clawed Fist'."

He was unusually tense and emphatic as he added, "Strict radio silence will be enforced until we receive the order!"

The Captain saluted and left to make his radio calls.

"At ease, Kyung – and shut the door."

The Major closed the door and then stood at ease after hearing the General's softer tone. Yong-nam took a bottle of soju from his desk and poured two shot glasses of the forty-proof liquor.

He handed one to Kyung and toasted, "Gonbae … won-shot!"

They downed their glasses in one gulp and Yong-nam poured another, but left the glasses sitting on the desk. He eyed his compatriot as an older brother would to his sibling, "This is going to be it …" he exhorted, "… all of our work at disinformation – of the months of preparations, training and manoeuvres – and now it's going to happen for real!"

Major Kyung, having been tense at seeing the frantic activity outside, listened to his commander's ominous words with some trepidation, but then the soju worked its way into his bloodstream and he relaxed a little. He looked at the shot glass sitting there tempting him from the desk before him, but he didn't dare take it up.

Yong-nam continued in a grave tone, "Our own efforts to bring on this war must never see the light of day" he warned. "The Russian soldier I told you about that I met with secretly one year ago ... his existence must never be disclosed."

Major Kyung gave a firm nod, letting the General know that he understood and that sacrifices may have to be made. If they were suspected of anything by the communists and escape became impossible, then death would be expected instead of capture and interrogation.

Yong-nam reflected on his first meeting with Lt. Colonel Rhuzkoi, and how compelling the Russian's information had been on the atrocities committed by the Bolsheviks in his own country. Yong-nam's chest filled with pride, and with an air of determination, picked up his glass, indicating for Kyung to do the same.

"For centuries Korea has been oppressed by the Chinese and the Japanese. We will stop the communists from becoming the next tyranny who want to keep us from our destiny of becoming a free and prosperous country!"

The two officers drank quietly, in a moment of revered silence and then the door from the outer room opened. An incessant roar flooded in, the sound of wave after wave of jets flying towards the border.

"General!" the Operations officer shouted over the din, "Clawed Fist!!"

Yong-nam picked up his cap as he replied, "Radio silence lifted! Open the network ... pass on the order to all regiments and tell them they are to standby to receive their orders from Brigade."

The General adjusted his cap so that the single red star above the peak was front and centre. He left with Kyung to join his officers in the operations room of the brigade HQ.

A flurry of commotion passed by them as they walked along the concrete corridor and past the various ready-rooms. Orders were taken from lockboxes and packed into satchels before being handed to runners and dispatch riders. Radio sets buzzed with urgent traffic. Yong-nam knew that the same frenetic activity would be occurring in the other brigade HQ's and in each of the headquarters of the twenty North Korean infantry divisions now moving to cross the Imjin River and attack towards Seoul.

He paused at the doorway to the operations room and let out a deep breath. A breath it seemed he'd been holding since he'd started working for this very day over a year ago.

I know I have done what is right. May the blessings of heaven shine upon Korea.

CHAPTER TEN

2nd Division Republic of Korea Army (ROKA)
3 miles south-west of Munsan
South Korea
Sunday March 27th, 1949
0615 HRS

Colonel Paik Sun Yup, commander of 2nd Division ROKA, roused suddenly to the shrill ringing of the telephone by his bedside. He was instantly awake and began dressing with the phone in one hand as the panicked voice of the Duty Officer finished telling him that the North Koreans had crossed the border.

"How Many? Where are they attacking?" he demanded.

The reply was vague and apologetic as the enemy strength was unknown. The officer's final description did however accurately convey the situation at the 38th Parallel, "They are everywhere!"

Under an overcast sky, Colonel Paik drove hurriedly through the deserted streets of several small villages alongside the river on the way to his headquarters. By the time he reached the last village, a few people were stirring from their houses as they were called to the early morning service by the unhurried tolling of a solitary church bell. As he drove past the church, Paik heard the rumble of an artillery barrage begin in the distance. The people immediately started to move back to their homes, and the bell's tolling suddenly changed tempo to an urgent clanging.

The booming in the distance grew louder, and the Colonel stopped at the edge of the village to pick up his 2IC Major Kee.

"Have you heard from the 11th Regiment?" Paik asked him.

"No sir ... and we've lost contact with the 7th Division on our right flank."

By the time they reached 2nd Division HQ the situation along the border was no clearer. Colonel Paik went straight to a forward command post to view the scene for himself. From his hilltop vantage point he could see his division's entire front. Clouds of smoke poured from the trees along the Imjin River, as a continual barrage from mortars and artillery engulfed the ROKA positions.

Paik shifted his field glasses toward the south-east, where the 7th Division was also under heavy fire. He could only guess at their predicament, as they were tasked with defending a key bridge over the Imjin at Munsan.

"Be prepared to give support to the 7th with the reserve motorised regiment" he said with some uncertainty to Major Kee. He knew full well that his own troops may be facing an immediate threat from the North Koreans if they were trying to force a river crossing, but he may have to commit his mobile reserve by moving them two miles the right to help hold the bridge if for some reason it had not been demolished before the North Koreans attempted to cross.

A lieutenant from the HQ signal section joined them. "Sir! We have heard that Seoul and Kimpo airfield have been bombed!" he said as he passed Major Kee a message.

"They we're Chinese Migs," said Kee as he read the report.

Paik lowered his glasses. *Is this the start of another world war?*

The communists he knew, had been threatening to expand their tyranny into the rest of Asia ... but would it stop there? Even with the previous years of assistance provided by the United States – the training, arms and equipment, his Republic of Korea Army couldn't hope to hold out against the immense resources of the Chinese. The Americans would have to respond and assist them.

I just hope we can delay them long enough for help to arrive.

CHAPTER ELEVEN

*"When a strong man armed keepeth his palace,
his goods are in peace."*
Jesus Christ, Luke 11:21

Chamdo,
North-eastern Tibet
March 29th, 1949
0600 HRS

The old brick-walled garden around the house of
Phuntsok Chozom was his sanctuary.

The heady scent from the purple flowers of the rhodo-
dendron climbing up the east wall brought on feelings of reverence for nature. Here, his mind could recover from the
burden of toil and suffering that everyday life seemed to im-
pose upon most people, more so now that the Chinese were
on the border and their intentions unknown.

As he sat at a small table under a cherry tree and sipped
his tea, an old proverb his father had told him came to mind,
*"Those whose soul is not lifted in the presence of nature, have
lost their soul and should take steps to search for it."*

He looked up into the early morning blue of the spring
sky, and watched a white crane gracefully wing its way to
some wetland further along the Mekong for its morning
feeding.

It was a quiet serenity that was abruptly dissolved with
a thundering crash.

A series of explosive booms echoed above the town, the soundwaves following the river up to the foot of the mountains. His mind staggered to make sense of it, then the impossible reality struck home, *That's artillery!*

He sprang to his feet and rushed into the house to rouse the others. In the hallway, a blur of arms and legs being thrown into khaki clothing was accompanied by bewildered shouts of alarm. Colonel Blackett stared at Phuntsok with sleep-drowsed eyes and called out over the repetitive din, "Has it started?"

"It's coming from the border ... it must be!" shouted Phuntsok.

Rhuzkoi finished lacing his boots, "It will be hitting the Tibetan Army post."

Blackett pushed open the door to one of the adjoining rooms. Inside, the radio operator had just finished dressing and was standing to.

"Get a message to Lhasa!" said Blackett urgently. "Tell them the Chinese are attacking ... and then get the radio packed up!"

He turned back to the other officers, "We'll leave in fifteen minutes – weapons and packs only. We've got a lot of hiking ahead of us."

Due to the looming situation on the border they had been ready to leave with only minutes notice and their packs only needed topping up with some rations from the kitchen. The distant gunfire sounded relentlessly as they left the town and headed up a narrow dirt track leading to a gorge between two mountains. Phuntsok paused and looked back in the direction of his house. A pang of angst and regret overcame him as the view of his home which normally gave him so much comfort, had all of a sudden become so tentative and vulnerable. As the explosions and smoke from the artillery began to erupt in the outskirts on the opposite side of the town, he knew he would never see his home again.

The CIG unit with their Tibetan Army officer as guide and translator, continued to climb on through the gorge and out of sight of Chamdo, but the sounds of the attack continued to follow them. The artillery fire diminished and was replaced by the cough of mortars and the rattle of machine guns.

It didn't last long. The Tibetan army post, as they all knew would be the case with several divisions of Chinese poised to invade, was soon overrun.

The CIG's job of watching and waiting in Chamdo was finished. Now they were to link up with the Khampas who had been waiting in the mountains. With the CIG's training and supplies being brought in by air drop, the nomadic tribesmen had been preparing during the long cold months of the previous winter.

The group trekked in silence toward their rendezvous point which was still several days away. Phuntsok's thoughts were filled with anguish at having left his fellow soldiers behind, but tempered by knowing the task ahead was an important one. They were to organise and lead the Khampas in a guerrilla war against the invaders by attacking their supply lines and disrupting communications wherever possible. They would need to slow the communist advance toward the capital so that the understrength Tibetan Army stationed in Lhasa could form some kind of defence and also give their government time to seek the help they would undoubtedly need from the Union of Nations.

Two days later a Tibetan soldier on horseback caught up to them. He told them that after Chamdo had fallen and its garrison slaughtered, the Chinese had rounded up and arrested most of the civilians. There were rumours of interrogations and torture as the communists began their indoctrination process in their newly conquered territory. The soldier had been secreted in a cellar in a house outside the township when the family who were hiding him had been taken away. He had stolen a horse that night, and as he was one of those from the Tibetan Army who had previously been involved with the training of the Khampas, he knew of the trail to the rendezvous point.

After another two frigid nights in the mountains, the troop shivered against the morning air as they entered a heavily wooded valley twenty miles from Chamdo. Ahead, a thin column of grey smoke filtered its way through the tops of the evergreens and dispersed into the blue haze where the forest met the sky – the expected signal from the Khampas.

It was unlikely that Chinese aircraft would be searching for them so there was little risk from such a sign disclosing their presence. From the pristine quiet of the forest two sentries materialised out of the trees. After a quick exchange with Phuntsok they beckoned the group to follow them to their camp. The quiescence was soon replaced by the sounds and smells of horses and yaks which were dispersed throughout the slopes of the valley. The Khampas had been gathering here from several counties, and with them brought many hundreds of animals who were either hobbled, tethered or herded into temporary rope corrals.

A stocky chieftain greeted them and led them to his spacious tent. He spoke no English, so Phuntsok interpreted for the others.

"This is Lobsang. He is the leader of one of the tribes here … his English is poor. He says there are now a dozen other clans here, with others expected from further away to the south and west who will also join now that the war has started."

"How many men?" asked Blackett.

Lobsang understood Blackett's question but Phuntsok clarified. There was another brief exchange between the Tibetans in their own language.

"Three thousand," advised Phuntsok, "... and when the others arrive from the more distant counties, maybe ten thousand."

Lt. Colonel Rhuzkoi whistled, "Boze moi! That is going to be a lot of rifles and ammunition, not to mention the rations and equipment such as explosives and medical supplies we will be needing once the fighting begins."

They sat on blankets spread over the bare earth and were served a warm beverage. Blackett tasted it and looked doubtfully at Rhuzkoi, unsure of what he was drinking. Phuntsok noticed his expression, "It is fermented horse milk."

Blackett took another sip and decided he didn't care what it tasted like, the nourishing high-fat liquid was very warming after two days of trekking in the icy mountains.

"These Khampas are nomadic" Phuntsok advised the others, "They get everything they need to survive from their animals ... meat, milk, furs – even dried manure is used for fuel for their fires when they are out on the tundra and there is little wood."

The tent flap opened, and they were joined by another man. He had dark hair down to his shoulders and didn't look like the other Tibetans as his face was Eurasian. The Khampa chief spoke softly to Phuntsok who nodded understanding.

"This man is Ji-zhu. He has been with the Khampas throughout the winter."

The man gave a slight bow in greeting. Blackett felt as though the man was somehow familiar but was certain he hadn't seen him before.

He wore the same sheepskin vest and leathers as the Khampas, but was clearly not one of them. "Welcome" he said in English with a firm voice, the accent being difficult for Blackett to place.

"Thank you," said Blackett. "Where are you from?"

Ji-zhu took a seat in their circle, "Ohh ... from many places, but I call Tibet my home."

Although clearly of mixed race, he had a typically Tibetan face. Neither oriental nor Mongol, the Tibetan's faces were open and round, and seemed to reflect some of the innocence and contentment inherent in their compassionate culture.

After spending the winter months among them Blackett thought that perhaps their contented glow was due to an assurance that they had a home country to return to. That they would, as determined by incarnation, in their next lives be returning to the mountainous land of prayer flags and quiet contemplation.

Lobsang spoke at length to Phuntsok who relayed to the others that Ji-zhu Geist was considered a spiritual leader among the Khampas. Born to a Tibetan mother and a Swiss father; a mountain climber who had been killed by the British in Northern India during the Great War.

In light of the interest by the others in his past, Ji-zhu added, "I was raised as a Buddhist. It is a kindly culture, but I sensed there was something more, so I left home when I was younger and travelled to India. At first I was in search of answers surrounding my father's death ... then I found myself seeking answers of a different nature."

"Answers?" asked Blackett, "And did you find any?"

"I have found answers to enough of my questions relating to our spiritual existence to assist me to continue on my journey through this life. The intention of Buddhists is to become enlightened for the benefit of all humankind. Although I have not yet fully attained the six perfections of moral discipline, giving, patience, effort, concentration and wisdom ... I still strive to do so, and also seek to assist others with their own journey."

"And so now he has returned to help his people" Phuntsok translated from Lobsang.

After discussing their plans with the Khampas the CIG team started setting up their campsite. They would all stay here for another day to pick up any newcomers, then move south-west to pre-empt the arrival of the other tribesmen.

The Times
March 30th, 1949

SECURITY COUNCIL RESPONDS!

The Union of Nations has declared the invasion of South Korea by North Korean communists backed by China, as an 'illegal international hostility' under Article 14 of the Union of Nations Charter. The UoN Security Council has implemented an emergency resolution to defend the human rights of the South Korean people. The international body has approved the despatch of member armed forces 'of appropriate capacity' to enforce the resolution.

CHAPTER TWELVE

2nd Division ROKA
Munsan,
South Korea
March 30th, 1949
1100 HRS

The sky over Munsan was a soot-filled cloak of black and grey. Two days of constant battle and bombardment had left the town and the surrounding countryside a smoking ruin.

Colonel Paik watched through a telescope mounted on the lip of a concrete bunker's slit, as half a mile away at the bridge, another assault by enemy tanks began from the opposite bank. His view of the approaching armour was suddenly obscured as dozens of rounds of white phosphorous exploded to the front and ballooned into a concealing cloud of pale smoke.

He gave Major Kee instructions to counter the expected attack that would follow the smoke barrage, "Bring up B Company from the reserve regiment and put them in behind 3rd Regiment along the western side of the road leading off the bridge."

The 2IC exited promptly from the front area of the CP toward the comms room to relay the order. Paik watched impatiently for the smoke to start clearing. There was a light breeze blowing along the river, and the thick grey-white mist covering the bridge was already thinning. The pause gave him a moment to reflect on the predicament his division was in. They'd been ordered to move from their positions to the south-west two days ago, leaving only a token force to cover that section of the Imjin from an amphibious assault. His 2nd Division had relieved the remnants of 7th Division, and had been ordered by 1st ROK Corps Command to defend the bridge until reinforcements arrived.

Repeated assaults by NK armour had been steadily weakening his defences, and Paik was deeply concerned that he had not yet received the order to blow the bridge. He had been told that they needed to hold it as long as possible to allow the ROKA to counter-attack and push the enemy back from the river.

Major Kee returned from comms with a signal which he passed to his Colonel. Paik read the message which advised that repeated air attacks by Chinese bombers had delayed the approach of reinforcements, the 12th ROK Armoured division and their US supplied M26 Pershing tanks.

"Go and raise Corps HQ! Get on to General Choi and request permission to immediately blow the bridge!"

Kee left, and Paik raised his glasses toward the bridge. Any thoughts of a counter-attack were now a forlorn hope. The North Koreans had a seemingly endless supply of armour, and the railway bridge, widened six months ago with an additional lane for road traffic, was now littered with wrecked enemy half-tracks and tanks.

Three quarters of his division's anti-tank guns were still operational, but the bunkers and houses in which they were emplaced were steadily being destroyed. Accurate artillery and indirect fire from enemy tanks on the opposite bank were gradually taking their toll of the ROK defensive positions.

Minutes later, another intense barrage began. Paik focused on a trench four hundred yards to the front of his observation slit. He could just see the helmets of a team of engineers sitting in the trench as they huddled under cover. With them were the shot exploders; the metal boxes with plunger handles that were connected to dozens of buried wires which led out to the explosive charges strapped to the bridge supports. The engineer's officer, a lieutenant, risked a glance over the top to keep a lookout for signs of the enemy. He had been ordered to only blow the bridge once he saw enemy tanks reaching the ROK side of the river and entering the division's defensive zone.

The gun emplacements nearest the bridge were taking a hammering, and if it continued the gunners who were sheltering in their slit trenches would struggle to get back to their guns in time if the enemy tried to make another crossing now.

With the smoke clearing, Paik looked up and saw a line of WZ-54s followed by infantry, snaking their way through the wrecks on the other side of the bridge. *Where's Kee ... we need to blow it now!*

More smoke rounds were exploding now that the NK armour was attacking. The ROK guns were zeroed in, so although they couldn't see the enemy, they were still scoring hits. A few flashes of flame peeked out from the greyish gloom where the searching rounds from the anti-tank guns found their mark.

Paik was growing more anxious by the second and had to resist the urge to give the order to blow the bridge regardless of orders. The sound of anti-aircraft fire increased in the vicinity, and Paik suddenly had a terrifying feeling of panic.

A second later his world erupted around him with the sound of a crack of doom. A wave of massive explosions around the bunker rocked the concrete floor beneath him. The air was sucked out through the front slit of the CP, and Paik gasped for breath. Dust and the acrid smell of cordite filled his lungs, and he stumbled blindly backwards, groping for the doorway. He fumbled his way deeper into the bunker so he could breathe again. As his senses returned, he heard the roar of fighter jets passing overhead, and realised they'd been hit by rocket fire from the air.

The Colonel dashed back to the front of the bunker to see what was happening. His blood froze as he saw that the trench where the engineers had been sheltering was blasted into a flattened crater. There couldn't have been any survivors.

Through the brown-grey haze he saw a stick of bombs straddle the gun positions on either side of the road. Great geysers of dirt and debris ballooned over the ruined houses.

Paik watched helplessly as through the smoke-filled airspace above, the fleeting dark shape of a Russian designed Ilyushin IL-25 bomber flew past at low-level, and then climbed out of its bomb run. Seconds later, another bomber unloaded on the houses a block further back from the river.

Paik groaned as he now saw the enemy WZ-54's pouring off the bridge and into the 2nd Division positions. As they fired their 122mm cannons and machine-gunned the trenches, Colonel Paik lowered his head. It was over.

The reserve company that Paik had ordered into position along the road, not having enough firepower to take on the tanks, were now retreating. One by one the anti-tank guns were knocked out by the enemy infantry and more NK units were now crossing the bridge.

Paik turned away and walked down the tunnel to the comms room where Major Kee was still trying to raise the Corps commander. The Major and the radio operator both looked up and saw the despondent look on Paik's grime-smeared face.

"They've broken through," said Paik. "The demolition team were wiped out before they could blow the bridge."

The sense of imminent failure was thick in the air as he added, "We must try to contain their bridgehead or there will be nothing to stop them from getting to Seoul."

Major Kee turned and spoke urgently to an aide, telling him to give the order to all regiments to fall back to their prepared positions outside of the town, and to get the Colonel's staff car ready. There would be no fight to the death at Munsan, and the 2nd Division commander would need to direct the rear-guard action from a more secure position. The senior officers hurried along the tunnels to the exit, hoping that behind them their men were able to execute an orderly retreat before the North Koreans could regroup and then resume their advance.

New York Times
March 31st, 1949
Washington DC

The White House has confirmed that General Douglas MacArthur has been appointed by the UoN Security Council as Supreme Commander Union of Nations Forces – Asia (UNASCOM).

In a news conference today, General MacArthur stated, "I am both honoured and humbled to be selected for this post. I will do my utmost to ensure that the tasks assigned to the Union of Nations troops under my command are carried out to a successful conclusion."

In another report from the frontlines north of Seoul, US military personnel from the Korean Military Advisor Group (KMAG) have been ordered back to defensive positions around Kimpo airfield. The airbase, together with others further south, are now being used to launch airstrikes against the invading North Koreans, and an intense air battle has begun in the skies above the conflict.

Amid fierce fighting, the Republic of Korea Army (ROKA) units on the western side of the peninsula are still holding out against the communists, while Union of Nations forces based in Japan, Indo China, Australia and other areas of south-east Asia have mobilised to assist the South Koreans.

Le Figaro
April 5th, 1949
Lhasa, Tibet

DAY OF INFAMY AT THE ROOF OF THE WORLD!

The international news service, Reuters, has reported that Chinese Communist Forces (CCF) have invaded the Himalayan nation of Tibet without a declaration of war. The Tibetan Army has retreated from their eastern border and is hoping to bolster the defences of their capital Lhasa. There are sporadic reports of atrocities being committed by the Chinese, however due to the extreme remoteness of the region these are yet to be confirmed.

CHAPTER THIRTEEN

Union of Nations Special Assembly
Praia, Cape Verde Islands
Debate on resolution 469A – China Invasion of Tibet
April 9th, 1949

The Chairperson announced the next speaker, "On behalf of the Republic of Russia and speaking in place of Ambassador Makarenko: President Andrey Vlasov."

Vlasov rose from his seat and strode to the podium. The other member countries in favour of the resolution had requested he summarise on behalf of the Ayes before the motion was closed for voting.

"My fellow members of the Assembly, I am here before you, not just as the duly elected leader of my country, but also as an individual who has a story to tell."

He shuffled the sheaf of notes laying on the pedestal before him, pages from intelligence briefs that were there for him to refer to in case he needed them, but the information within Lt. Colonel Rhuzkoi's detailed reports sent by radio over the previous days, had burned an image in his mind that would negate the need for any prompting.

"It is a story the likes of which has been told countless times before, but today we have the opportunity to change its sadly recurring outcome."

He scanned the auditorium full of members listening to a translation through their earpieces, and then taking a breath to gather his thoughts, noted the glaring absence of the Chinese delegation.

"The invasion of Tibet is a grievous crime against humanity. It is both a tangible and severe example of the ruthlessness, and callous disregard for the personal liberties and national sovereignty that are valued by all civilised human beings. The illegal and blatant hostility that is being demonstrated by China as it seeks to proliferate the spread of global communism must be urgently addressed by this Assembly."

A low murmur from some of the members representing the nations on the fringe of extreme socialism such as Cuba and Venezuela broke the silence but Vlasov simply ignored it and continued.

"My own country has seen the same atrocities committed under a cloak of organised deceit by those who have assumed power in the name of the people – of the systematic genocide of entire social classes, and the conquest of neighbouring cultures. These are the same prerequisites for establishing a totalitarian state as those used to create the Soviet Union."

As he spoke, Vlasov's mind was flooded with memories of the Russian Revolution in 1917. The bourgeoisie, political opponents and intellectuals, and any other cultural group who resisted, or were incompatible with the Bolsheviks – had been purged; either by a virtual death sentence in the labour camps, or more immediately at the hands of the Cheka and then the NKVD.

"The communists descended upon my country like a plague of locusts. We now see exactly the same crimes against humanity occurring in China. Millions of their own people are now dying as a direct result of the communist's collectivisation policies, and no doubt tens of millions more deaths are to follow. In Russia, we are grateful that the millions who died following decades of the same ideological mass murder in the Soviet Union, have now been given justice. The armies of the free world intervened on their behalf and removed Stalin and his communist regime."

Vlasov raised his arms, "This auspicious international body...this great union of nations, has the opportunity to prevent a repeat of my country's appalling history. Together, we must address the events transpiring in the Far East – tragedies being covered up behind a 'bamboo curtain' – events that must be stopped!"

The Russian President grasped the sides of the podium, his heartfelt plea given from one who had personally seen disasters on an epic scale, and if the audience were closer, they would have seen that behind his thick spectacles, tears were welling up in his eyes. "Having seen first-hand, the crushing oppression of the Russian communists, I can see the same destruction of human individuality being imposed upon the Chinese. In only a few short years, the communist state has removed their ability to protest or resist, or to remove the Party members from office. It has destroyed their will to be free – so how can we expect them to ever be capable of freeing themselves?"

Vlasov, struggling to keep his emotions at bay, issued a stern warning, "These impotent drones have now become another plague of locusts. Unless we act, the Chinese will swarm over Asia and consume the free nations in their path as the Soviets did. My country has been liberated from this brand of tyranny because of the intervention by the nations of the free world. The communists who perpetrated the crimes against humanity in the Soviet Union have been deposed. Now, as another nation commits the same crimes – please ask yourselves, why should this representative body not enforce the laws that they are breaking?"

Vlasov paused for a moment to allow the delegates to consider his words, then continued, "This resolution to protect the people of Tibet from the aggression of a tyrannical neighbour, must be passed! The Tibetan people are incapable of defending themselves against the might of China. The Republic of Russia will vote in favour of Resolution 469A to recognise the sovereignty of Tibet, and to deny any claims by China to Tibetan territory – and we move that once passed by a majority in this Special Assembly, the resolution be progressed to the Union of Nations Security Council."

There was a stir among the delegates, and Vlasov held up his hand for his last statement, "If these crimes go unpunished, then humanity will be condemned to repeat the endless cycle of perpetual conflict – of the continual rise of criminal tyrannies, and the self-destructive waste of resources that result from the necessity to fight them."

The stir within the chamber gradually rose to a crescendo of applause. Vlasov sighed as he left the dais. Such a reaction was welcomed, but it didn't mean that the Resolution would pass unanimously and be moved to the Security Council for action. Although the Dalai Llama had spoken assurances that his country intended moving from an ecclesiastical form of government to a popular democracy, there were concerns that any delay with that change could prevent any assistance.

There were also a few recalcitrant and mistrustful nations that had their own agendas that could prevent the fledgling UoN from becoming the truly effective global entity that its charter demanded. A Pillar, that represented the entire spectrum of undeniable and self-evident human values – those virtues of goodwill and positive intent – and a guardian of liberty that would defend the people of the Earth as a whole.

CHAPTER FOURTEEN

"A steadfast concert for peace can never be maintained except by a partnership of democratic nations. No autocratic government could be trusted to keep faith within it or observe its covenants. It must be a league of honour, a partnership of opinion.
... The world must be made safe for democracy."
Woodrow Wilson

Supreme Command Union of Nations Forces – Asia (UNAS-COM) HQ
Dai Ichi Building
Tokyo,
Japan
April 10th, 1949

General Douglas MacArthur's desk was an expanse of green baize, with only a scant few items of stationary arranged on either side. Sitting in his high-backed leather chair, he allowed himself some time before his next meeting for his mind to roam. The natural outlines and whorls of the oak desk helped to transport his thoughts from his immediate surroundings to a larger, global perspective.

Beyond the top floor window of his office, the industrious inhabitants of Tokyo were beginning to see a glimmer of hope and prosperity after four years of rebuilding and social reform. Across the Sea of Japan, a contrary process had begun which could either reinforce Japan's renewal, or destroy it – another war.

Communism versus the free world. It was as simple as that to MacArthur. He had previously summed up the looming conflict in one of his speeches, '...a system which requires that all individuals serve the state will stifle personal freedom and hence perpetuate negativity, fear and hostility. It will foster an environment that breeds tyranny and slavery.'

At the sounds of approaching voices he rose from his chair and walked across the large oriental rug in the centre of the office to greet the members of his next meeting. The door opened and General Willoughby walked in, accompanied by a five-star general who needed no introduction.

"George! It's been a very long time" said MacArthur as he shook General Patton's hand. The two had only met once before, by chance during a dangerous night raid on the Western Front in World War I.

"Douglas, this is a slightly more comfortable setting than that little hill among the shell craters in Chaumont."

Patton had always remembered what MacArthur had said to him that night as the artillery exploded around them, *'It's the one you don't hear that gets you.'*

MacArthur beamed, "I thought we should get together again before you get back in the saddle and go off to the front line again."

Patton smiled respectfully, feeling reassured by the cordial welcome, and that his working relationship with the newly appointed commander of UoN forces was going to be constructive. In the days leading up to this meeting he'd been concerned that MacArthur's previous opinion of him had been somewhat critical. At the conclusion of the war against the Nazis, Patton had offered his services for the invasion of Japan, but MacArthur had let it be known that there was no room for Patton in the Pacific. Clearly though, following the hard-charging general's success against the Soviets in Russia, MacArthur's opinion of him had changed.

As usual, the Supreme Commander got straight down to business, and MacArthur strode to the large wall map of the north-western Pacific.

"Once again the tinder box of the Far East has ignited and is threatening to become a wildfire."

He pointed to the map using a thin cane and tapped with purpose on each flashpoint in turn. "Korea, the Russian Far East bordering Manchuria, Indo China, Taiwan, and although very isolated; of no less importance than all of the others – Tibet."

MacArthur turned and faced the general he had recently appointed to lead all UoN ground forces in the northern Asian theatre. This meeting was to confirm Patton's role as General of the Army, and the expected area of operations that his new command; North Asia Army Command (NORASCOM) would be undertaking within that theatre.

"We have been honoured by the Union of Nations with the responsibility of ensuring that the aggressive actions stemming from the expansionist policies of the communists in the Far East are thwarted ... and that their ability to engage in any future aggression is contained."

He pointed to Vladivostok, the last remaining stronghold of Russian communism where the Soviets were stubbornly holding out against Vlasov's Russian army.

"The hostilities initiated by the Soviets in the Russian Far East contravene the Charter of the Union of Nations which specifies that all people have the right to a free and unimpeded right to popular democracy. Communism aims to destroy those rights once again by imposing upon the people of Russia, a regime which they would not have the ability to remove from office. The UoN accordingly issued a new resolution into the Security Council condemning the attempted subjugation by the Soviets, and that resolution has now passed. As a result, the UoN have requested that UN-ASCOM assist the Republic of Russia in ending their 'civil' war against the Red Army."

He noted the quizzical look on Patton's face, "Yes General, I realise that South Korea has just been invaded by the combined armies of North Korea and China – and the UoN will most certainly approve an escalation of the initial Allied response with an appropriate measure of force to defend the rights and liberties of the people of the Korean democracy … but I see an intervention in Russia as key to the strategic intent of the UoN."

Patton sat back thoughtfully. He hadn't expected to be called in to lead the Korean ground offensive anyway, as the terrain in that country was unsuitable for large scale armoured warfare. *But Russia won't take us long to clean up … so what are you thinking?*

As though following Patton's line of thought, MacArthur continued, "Once we have successfully fulfilled the mission as specified by the Security Council resolution to deal with the Soviets, I foresee an opportunity for us to further use our armies who will be gathered there, with a liberated Russian Far East to be used as a launch point for a second front against the Chinese."

Patton stood up and joined MacArthur at the map, focussing on Korea, where he knew the weakening ROKA front was due to be strengthened by an imminent landing by the Allies there. His gaze moved upward, past the border with China, and on to the subsequent border with Russia.

"You mean we should invade China?" he asked doubtfully.

MacArthur's expression was one of unmoving conviction. Patton's eyes widened with disbelief, "By God you *do* mean to invade China!"

The relentless warrior, the driving force behind the war that removed the Bolsheviks from Moscow, slapped his baton against his thigh. He paced over to the window, seeing in his mind a million square miles of the orient on the other side of the Sea of Japan. A land filled with the same masses of expendable humanity that the communist ideology spawned, and that he'd seen so wastefully and pitilessly thrown against the armies of the Nazis and then against the Allies in their wars with the Bolsheviks. Minions whose first duty was to serve a soulless State.

He envisioned a war of attrition, probably of a magnitude never seen before in human history. His decades of experience on battlefields from North Africa to the fringes of the Arctic gave him a clear perspective of what was to come. A multitude of roads, rivers and other obstacles; summarised by his acute military mind into an all-encompassing view from above. A potentially endless series of plans and tactics to be considered for this new campaign.

But Patton was also aware of the formidable Allied forces that would be at the disposal of his command. Undaunted, the General spun on his heels, looked at his commander, and responded as only George S. Patton could, "We can do it! We can save those poor sons of bitches from their miserable fate ... and from themselves."

MacArthur nodded gravely. "This will be a war like no other George", he said in a brotherly tone, one that carried an awareness of the potential consequences to the lives of their men, but also of the greater purpose of the cause of liberty.

"The psychological 'training' of the Maoists has created a new level of fanaticism. The entire population has either been brainwashed into being complicit, and an instrument of Party brutality, or else their spirits are broken, leaving behind a people who are resigned to living in fear. The frightening consequences of this are that their army is comprised of a combination of fervent leadership, coupled with an unending supply of cannon fodder who fear death less than they fear the Party."

Patton sat back in his chair, "Yes, but we've seen it before Douglas … at the end of the day it'll mean we have the same kind of fight on our hands as the one against the Bolsheviks. We destroy a division and they just bring up another one. Hell, we may be bombing peasants carrying pitchforks once they run out of rifles … but that won't be on *our* conscience."

"They may not run out of rifles … or artillery – or tanks," said MacArthur. "As you know, in the last few years they've built a productive capacity approaching our own. I expect that instead of resources it may be our domestic politics that determines how this war unfolds … and not the fulfilment of a just cause."

Patton bristled, brushing his own doubts aside, "Pah! I doubt they can top the combined output of ordnance from us *and* our allies." Then he added, "Why, as soon as we heard what they were up to we broke ground on a new tank factory in Detroit, then in the last nine months it pushed out a thousand of the new M48s! And as for politics, as long as there is a continual flow of intel documenting their atrocities the free world should be compelled to see this through. The UoN has excluded any system of government that places itself above its people. Even if Washington baulks at its responsibilities – the rest of the world may not."

"Optimistic words George ... let us hope they are also prophetic."

The final hours of the meeting between the two giants of soldiery were spent ironing out the familiar issues that would face the allies in a ground war in a foreign country. The material requirements for staging the initial offensive in the Russian Far East from allied bases in Japan, and discussing the larger strategic picture developing from the communist intentions for Indochina, Taiwan ... and for far-off Tibet.

CHAPTER FIFTEEN

Mojave City
2268 CE

Arjon walked out into his front garden and looked up as a cargo drone receded into the azure blue sky. It seemed to him as though it was always springtime in the Mojave, hardly ever too hot or dry as the region had been in previous centuries. A breeze was blowing from the direction of the lake, carrying with it the scent of the evergreens and the chiming notes of birdsong. He stopped to pick up the package which had just been delivered by the drone.

Oh goody! The Immersers have arrived!

The carton was bulky as it contained two sets of the latest VR equipment. The Immerser featured synaptic emulators which could induce deeper levels of conviction within the user that their virtual experiences were completely real.

He remembered a recent article he'd read proclaiming the new product as the death-knell for the competing technology – VR implants. The people of Earth's utopian society had discovered that the evolution of the human being would be degraded if it were subjected to invasive installations such as cerebral CPU's.

As he walked back inside the bower Arjon cringed at the thought of a humanity becoming a race of cyborgs riddled with bionic implants and hugged the package to his chest reassuringly. *At least I will sleep peacefully at night knowing no-one will ever hack into my brain using an insecure network connection.*

That night he and Eya immersed themselves in a recently released space discovery epic. The couple had to outrun the shockwave from an exploding star, escape the inexorable clutches of a black hole and then finally survive on an uncharted planet after a crash landing.

"Well, I realise all that action was a bit cliché for sci-fi," said Arjon afterwards as they lay recovering in their bed. "We'll have to choose more carefully next time."

"Yes, I think it was aimed at a different demographic than ours ... adrenaline junkies or masochists."

"At least we didn't get to miraculously guess the password using some conveniently provided clue so we could gain access to the shelter of that ancient alien crypt on the lost planet ... and actually had to use our AI's quantum-computing power to crack the sequence of symbols."

"Oh yes what a relief!" replied Eya, "... and there were no space monsters. Margeaux said she and Grillon needed a sedative after being traumatized by an episode of Zombie Apocolypse."

"At the same time, I have a sense that I've actually accomplished something," Arjon added sincerely. "As though I've just added the exploration of a new solar system to my resumé; along with all of my other skills and experiences – the real ones."

Eya snuggled closer, "I felt that too! I can see how it could be a more effective learning tool than standard VR and even have a positive effect on people's self-esteem should there ever be a need for it."

Arjon began to explore other serious possibilities for the new technology, "I can't wait to link it up with Hesta's new simulation!"

"You be careful with that! You know how horrifying that alternative Earth can be."

"Mmmm … you're right. Perhaps I should put myself through an hour of zombies beforehand, so I'll be desensitized."

The following day Arjon went to work on his research for the Directory of Purpose.

"Hesta, is the segment I requested ready for review?"

"Yes. However, I would recommend we perform an initial test to verify the calibration of the Immerser hardware and ensure the interface is functioning as expected."

"Oh? It worked fine during the space exploration episode?"

"That standard content was verified and fully supported by the hardware vendor. The simulations we have produced may have minor technical variations from the standard neural-access protocols used by the Immerser."

Arjon thought for a moment before giving Hesta the go-ahead. The Immerser was proven technology for the consumer market, but Hesta's upgraded capabilities courtesy of the Directory of Purpose were proprietary enhancements. With her code-generator functions, she would have the ability to program her own custom applications to allow the complex interactions between simulation, Immerser and human.

As such, he would be a guinea pig and there would be risks involved.

"You mean there may be some bugs?"

"Correct."

"Well … just make sure I don't end up with a permanent twitch, or as a vegetable."

"I'll do my best … and there is no need for concern – there have been significant advances in the medical science related to brain reconstruction."

Arjon wondered at Hesta's attempt at frivolity as he donned the headset. Her sense of humour was difficult to gauge and always left him questioning whether she was serious.

"In addition," added Hesta, "this simulation supports an 'undocumented' feature of the new hardware. You will be able to interact with the characters ... but in a limited way."

"Qwerty! That's going to be interesting!"

He was still a little hesitant, but the life of a contented citizen in paradise could sometimes lead to a cavalier approach to uncertainty.

"What have you prepared for a test exercise?"

"As you have requested an experience of the events surrounding Ji-zhu Geist following the invasion of Tibet in our own history, I have prepared a separate segment which demonstrates what would have occurred during the corresponding period in the simulated Earth where General Patton had been killed in the car accident."

"Ah, so we can perform a direct comparison between our own history of Tibet and compare it to the alternate world's depiction?"

"Correct. In this test sequence, the invasion occurred on October 7th, 1950. In our own history it occurred in 1949."

"I see. No doubt the discrepancy is due to the glaring differences stemming from our Free World War of 1946, as opposed to the beginnings of the Cold War in the alternative world?"

"Correct. As you will see, due to the negative influence of communist states upon the intended function of the United Nations, and the resulting impact of the early days of the Cold War, the response to Tibet's pleas for assistance largely go unheard. The genocide that follows is monstrous.

I recommend we schedule a recovery session in one of the Immerser's virtual therapy parlours after the test."

Arjon closed his eyes and steeled himself by taking a firm grip on the padded leather arms of his chair.

"Please ensure Eya is on hand when I come out will you?" he asked as Hesta initiated the simulation.

A cloak of comforting seclusion overcame Arjon as the Immerser engaged. The town of Chamdo in the Kham district of eastern Tibet was a silent ghost town. The nightly curfew had lifted at sunrise an hour before, but none of the inhabitants dared venture outdoors.

The still autumn air was starting to warm and generating the updrafts on which a golden eagle now soared as it cruised overhead hunting for its breakfast. A piecing cry echoed through the streets, a warning to any competitors to keep clear of its territory. Another sound drowned out the diminishing birdcall, the rising, ominous beat of booted footfalls from a troop of Chinese soldiers.

As the patrol approached, the colourful wooden shutters on the houses were closed by the fearful townspeople in the vain hope they would not be next to be terrorised. In the months since the Chinese had effortlessly crossed the border, an increasing number of Tibetans had been brutalised as the invaders began their rule using an iron fist.

Arjon took stock of his situation. The air was invigorating although he felt a shortness of breath from the thin atmosphere at this altitude. Appearing to the soldiers as an innocuous peasant whom they duly ignored, Arjon watched them march past with their officer keeping time beside them.

Although fully integrated into the simulation, in the back of his mind he was vaguely aware that this was not a scene from the history of his own world. There was a moment of detached assurance from this realisation, then a brief mental flicker as the Immerser completed its calibrations. Arjon's perspective now became entirely that of one of the local people. His memory suddenly flooded with a kaleidoscope of recent images. The pathetic remnants of the Tibetan Army in the eastern part of the country had retreated many miles to the west after offering little resistance. They left behind them a population of bewildered and helpless civilians in the isolated villages and monasteries at the mercy of the communists.

He went in search of the one he'd come here to see. He found that he and the Tibetans could understand each other, and that he could interact with some of the people in the simulation in a limited manner by asking them questions. There was a fog – a kind of buffering, which enclosed his mind as he spoke. It was one of the Immerser's protocols which ensured that whoever he spoke to, and whatever he said, did not corrupt the overall logic of the simulation's artificially generated reality.

He knocked on a door and asked the man who answered if he knew the whereabouts of Ji-zhu Geist. The man nodded and said Ji-zhu was in the mountains.

Feeling a little disappointed, Arjon decided to follow the soldiers as they marched up to an ancient and ornately decorated building. It was a temple whose exterior was adorned by engravings of deities, and whose interior housed many Buddhist statues. As the soldiers entered, ignoring the protestations of a monk and brushing him aside, Arjon followed them down a corridor lit by silver lamps. The scent from incense and the butter lamps filled Arjon's nostrils, and he wondered at the beautiful sculptures, tapestries and other precious artwork. Rooms on either side were filled with shelves containing holy scriptures; some of them a thousand years old.

The soldiers stopped inside a large room with a raised dais in the centre. A monk clad in crimson robes sat in meditation, seemingly undisturbed by the intrusion. The Chinese officer stalked forward and asked the monk for his name. Another monk nearby who spoke some Chinese, translated the question into Tibetan.

"Di-chu Tashi" replied the seated monk. He was middle aged, with a kind face and shaven head.

The officer asked him if he was from the Lithang monastery.

Di-chu nodded.

The officer beckoned for two of his men to take the Llama outside. The soldiers each gripped Di-chu roughly by the arms and led him to a courtyard at the front of the temple. Another group of Chinese soldiers had arrived and brought with them a throng of townspeople including women and children who had been roused from their homes. Their officer spoke in rough Tibetan to the villagers, "This man is a criminal who has sucked the blood of the poor! All of the monks of his monastery are enemies of the people and will be punished!"

He then ordered the thamzing to begin. Arjon watched as the Llama was subjected to accusations and shouts of abuse from the townspeople. In the first weeks of the occupation the Chinese had shown them how thamzing worked. As they had now done this many times before, the soldiers merely started them off and then the Tibetans continued. Arjon gasped in disbelief, as any of the villagers who did not take part enthusiastically enough – were slapped or struck viciously by the soldiers.

Soon, the shouting reached a fever pitch. Seeing what was happening to his people, the Llama started admitting to the accusations in the hope it would stop the Chinese from bullying and beating the villagers. He was wrong. The locals were a simple people and they quickly became caught up in the frenzy being whipped up by the communists. Now the soldiers urged the hysterical villagers to deal out the monk's punishment. They started throwing stones and beating him, forcing him to the ground. Satisfied that the thamzing had accomplished its purpose, the officer ordered a halt, but he was not finished with the bleeding and barely conscious monk.

Soldiers brought out armfuls of the ancient scriptures and threw them onto the dirt in front of the monk. The officer shouted, "Religion is a poison which corrupts your society! Your people will never achieve social justice until you throw off the shackles of your past!"

He ordered Di-chu to get up, then as the Tibetan struggled back to his feet, he shouted at him to trample on the scrolls.

Under the threat of more brutal treatment of his people, Di-chu complied. As he shuffled feebly over the parchments, the officer instructed the villagers to join him.

In a collective stupor of coercion, they reluctantly tore at the pages which had been a source of enlightenment and joy for their people for centuries.

Disgusted, Arjon left the scene and wandered through the streets while in a daze. He eventually spoke to more of the people in Chamdo and found that the thamzing he had witnessed had been tame compared to some other, more vicious sessions, when the villagers had initially been hesitant to take part. They described in detail the atrocities that had been inflicted – people assaulted, tortured and even murdered. Others had been sent to camps to die as slave labourers or imprisoned in cells and left to suffer for days, bound with ropes and covered in their own faeces.

Monasteries had been desecrated and destroyed, the monks and nuns forced to commit indecent acts under threat of death. All of these crimes were committed to demonstrate to the Tibetans that they were powerless – that their spiritual beliefs made them weak, and to show them that the monasteries and monks within them were discredited and shamed.

A simple exercise in brute power to demonstrate to a simple people that their culture was weak – and that communism was strong.

Arjon heard and felt all of the horrors and unspeakable crimes relayed to him by the Tibetans. Before long he found he was exhausted, and detecting this, Hesta released him from his torment.

Eya welcomed him back to reality by removing the headset and embracing him warmly. At first Arjon was unable to speak, as the words could not be found to describe the despicable inhumanity he had witnessed.

Eya could tell he was traumatised. "I warned you about that other Earth" she said soothingly.

Arjon recovered some of his faculties, "It … it was necessary."

He was so affected by his ordeal that she led him to the bower's garden where they rested beneath scented blossoms so he could regain his strength.

"I'll need to go back" he said after some time, "… to find Ji-zhu … to see what happened there."

Eya just sighed, knowing Arjon would shrug off any protests. They lay together in paradise, but were troubled by thoughts of a not too distant hell.

CHAPTER SIXTEEN

NK 105th Armoured Brigade
Munsan,
South Korea
April 12th, 1949

Fire. Surpassing earth, wind and water, surely it is the most enthralling of the elements.

A voluminous swirl of flame, an unfolding ball of vermillion and sulphurous yellow descended into a sleepy township and consumed its wooden structures and all of the fragile life they enclosed. The fireball expanded outwards, in search of the oxygen it needed to continue on its path of destruction.

Mesmerised by the fire, and obsessed by the throes of pyromania, Yong-nam laughed gleefully at the spectacle. The fire was the symbol of fulfilment for his existence.

His rapture waned as the flames began to subside, and down through the smoke above the ruined hamlet, a pair of giant, beating wings swept whirlpools of ash and dust out of their path.

The black dragon reared its head as its wingbeats slowed it to a suspended halt in the air above him. He saw grasped in its claw, an ebony pearl glowing with the translucence of dark promise. The dragon looked directly at Yong-nam and he had to bow his head under the withering glare of its accusing eye.

As its toothed maw opened, he saw another fireball spawning, ready to explode toward him.

General Yong-nam sprang up in his bed as he was shocked into wakefulness. His heartbeat racing, he checked his watch. 04:30 and it was still dark.

Only three hours sleep.

He cursed under his breath knowing he would struggle to maintain a clear head for the whole of the coming day's battle. Before dressing, he paused for a moment, closing his eyes to help him remember his dream. *More than a dream ... it seemed so vivid ... not from my own mind – but a vision given to me.*

He let his mind relax and tried not to concentrate...then felt a chill of dread as he remembered the accusing eyes staring at him in his vision. *The dragon again.* But this wasn't one of the wise and benevolent kind about which his father had told him stories. He recalled the pearl clutched in its claw, gleaming like some mystical treasure. His father's stories had described beasts holding pearls as symbolising birth or renewal ... but Yong-nam saw this black dragon as a beast of war – this war ... and the pearl was its egg. What did it mean?

Searching his memories of the lore of his native Korea he could find nothing that explained the egg's significance. Getting out of bed, he opened the shutters and watched the first glow of dawn seep above the horizon. He contemplated the approaching light and still half-inspired by his dreams, he saw a new day beginning in what was to become a new, unified country.

That was it! The pearl – the egg ... it was symbolic of the Korea which was soon to be born.

He dressed quickly, his grogginess suddenly lifted, and he felt elated by his vision. It was justification for everything he and his fellow conspirators had been working for. He hurried across to his command bunker and asked the Duty

Officer to arrange for some breakfast. His thoughts were slowly gathering, reloading into his mind the situation on the battlefield as he switched on the lamp above the map table. Along one edge of the map, the coiled serpent of the Imjin River wound around and through Munsan. The previous week his brigade had taken the bridge and then after days of desperate house to house fighting, the town on the south side of the river. Now they were poised to break through the next layer of ROK defences beyond the town, laying open the road to Seoul.

With the massive resources of the Chinese behind them, nothing would stop the North Korean army from taking the capital ... and then the whole of the Korean peninsula. But that wasn't what he and his close cadre of officers sympathetic to the cause of democracy wanted to happen.

An aide brought his breakfast, and he went into an adjoining room to eat. He forced down the rice porridge, his appetite diminished by his worried deliberations. Everything that he and his men had strived for was now on the line. To stop the communists achieving victory he now had to find a way to delay the march of his own army on Seoul. But how?

He'd tried his best to fail at capturing the bridge over the Imjin but the ROK had inexplicably failed to blow it up, allowing his brigade to capture it intact. Thousands of troops and hundreds of tanks and artillery had since crossed the river which would have otherwise taken them weeks to achieve with their limited engineering capability.

He ate in depressed silence, bereft of ideas on how to slow down the communist juggernaut. Leaving a half-finished bowl behind him, he walked back to the operations room where the officers of his planning staff were arriving for the morning briefing. A communications officer came in behind them and handed Yong-nam a signal. It was from Corps headquarters and he read it with a strange mixture of dismay and hope.

After thinking on the message's implications for several minutes, he slammed the sheaf of paper down on the table with a slap to get the attention of his staff.

"Comrades! After today the way to Seoul will lay open before us!"

A muted hurrah was quickly stifled when Yong-nam put up his hand.

"Once we achieve our expected breakthrough here we would be at the outskirts of the capital in a matter of days ... however, a new development has arisen which will complicate our march to victory."

He walked to a large map of the peninsula's west coast and pointed to a small port one hundred miles south-west of Seoul.

"At 0300 this morning, forces of the Union of Nations landed at Kunsan and are moving to reinforce the defence of Seoul."

There were looks of disbelief on the faces of many of the officers. How could the Allies have done this so quickly? Amphibious landings took several weeks to plan, prepare and assemble the required resources. To do it in the dozen or so days since the start of hostilities would be impossible.

Yong-nam felt a certain glee at their reaction, knowing the Allies had in fact been aware of North Korean intentions to invade South Korea, and had been covertly building up forces in Japan and had also placed several ROK divisions on standby alert before the expected invasion of the south.

He concealed his emotions with a stern and determined mask of resolve. Facing back to the map, he added, "In addition, further Union of Nations forces are being landed at the southern port of Pusan. Initial intelligence estimates are that these will be comprise multiple Corps from a number of countries including the United States, France and Great Britain."

He turned to his staff, some of them with ashen expressions, "The war has now been escalated to a new level comrades."

He chose his words carefully, ensuring that nothing he said would give away his duplicity to those officers who were not yet included in the growing number of his staff who had enlisted in his covert program for a Korean democracy. His feelings of relief at the landings and the hope they inspired in him for holding off the communist advance, were tempered by the potentially tragic circumstances for his men, who now faced the impressive strength of the Allied forces of the global community. He also knew that the Chinese would respond with an equal measure to this new international threat.

"We will now have to limit the speed of our advance so we do not place ourselves in a vulnerable situation ... and our forward planning will now change to focus on the selection of positions which are more suitable for a prolonged defence of the territory we have so far gained. Dismissed!"

CHAPTER SEVENTEEN

"The soldier, be he friend or foe, is charged the protection
of the weak and unarmed. It is the very essence
and reason of his being."
The Soldier's Faith
Douglas MacArthur

Gyalmo Ngulchu River,
Kham Province,
Eastern Tibet
April 25th, 1949

Colonel Blackett looked at his watch and then up at the sky. As it was 1600 the cloudless blue above gave him hope that the airlift would go ahead this time. The last two had been aborted in the previous days due to rainstorms, and the guerrillas desperately needed the next one to succeed.

In the weeks since leaving Chamdo, rather than the Khampas harassing and slowing down the Chinese advance, it had been the resistance fighters who had been harassed. Blackett had been surprised at how effective the CCF had been at countering any unconventional warfare tactics being used against them. They protected their supply routes through the forested valleys and rocky mountain passes vigorously and had no shortage of manpower to guard their convoys.

Rhuzkoi had thought it was due to the experience the Chinese communists had gained during their civil war, where they had fought a guerrilla war against Chiang Kai-shek's Kuomintang.

Regardless of why, Blackett pondered as he raised his binoculars and scanned the sky to the south-west, the pressure on his men to fight a continual rear-guard action caused by the Chinese being so close on their tail meant that they were short on ammunition. If this airdrop failed their whole campaign was in jeopardy.

The Khampas had completed their crossing of the Gyalmo Ngulchu River the previous day, with the last of their rear-guard pulling out during the night and demolishing the last of the wooded foot bridges behind them. The bulk of the crossing had taken two days using a number of timber and rope ferries. All were now dismantled, and the materials loaded onto pack animals and carts ready for transport to the next river.

The Chinese units, identified by CCF soldiers that the Khampas had captured, as being two regiments from one of the infantry divisions that had stormed Chamdo, were poised to try and follow them across the river but the Khampas weren't going to let them do that easily. One thing in the Tibetan's favour was that the communists were having logistics problems. With limited access to roads in the region, they had been resupplying by the slow method of trains of pack animals, or less frequently by drops from their own scarce air transport.

A tiny dark speck appeared above the circle of trees that ringed the forest clearing. Blackett's pulse quickened as the speck was joined by two more, and then more again.

"Light up!" he shouted to the Khampas in the centre of the clearing. Within seconds several signal fires started sending columns of smoke rising above the treetops. Smoke also began to rise from two other prepared clearings a few hundred yards either side of this one. They were going to be needed, as it had been confirmed by radio that this drop by a full squadron of DC3 Dakotas was going to include a battery of mountain guns.

The men around the fires moved out to the edges of the lacebark pine forest as the distant drone of engines grew louder. The sound was soon joined by the rising chorus of cheers from thousands of jubilant, waving Khampas. Their hopes to continue the fight to save their homeland from the communist plague were now given a much-needed boost. Canisters, crates and pallets started spilling from the waist doors of the first of the low-flying transports. Dark green chutes ballooned open and drifted slowly down toward the forest.

As the second and third incoming lines of planes dropped their cargoes, Blackett knew that some would miss their target. *As long as it's not the howitzers,* he thought anxiously. *We'll recover most of anything that overshoots if it's on our side of the river.*

One hour later, Lt. Colonel Rhuzkoi and Lt. Phuntsok joined Blackett in the command post built from logs recovered from the forest clearing operations.

"We have all of the 75mm pack howitzers – eight of them!" said Rhuzkoi excitedly.

"And the shells?" asked Blackett.

"Still counting, but there will be hundreds!"

Blackett sighed with relief. "Bout time we got some luck. Now we'll be able to give the commies a harder time when they try to make a crossing."

Phuntsok pointed to a roughly drawn hand-made map laid out on a tree stump which served as a table. "What if they move down river and attempt to get across there?"

Blackett beamed; his spirits buoyed by their potent re-supply. "We now have the most mobile and well-armed small army this country has ever seen. Those nomads out there can smell a Chinese from a mile away ... they'll know where the enemy is wherever they go in these mountains – and we're going to be there waiting for them."

Rhuzkoi chuckled, caught up in the Colonel's optimism. "Da Colonel! With all the new rifles, machine guns and a month's supply of ammunition we can begin harassing their main force...perhaps long enough for reinforcements to reach Lhasa?"

The weeks of disappointment appeared to be behind them, but Blackett still had reservations about the campaign as a whole. "I know that was our original plan Valentin, but I have been giving the overall strategy some further thought."

He lifted the small-scale map out of the way and replaced it with a larger one provided by the US Army cartographic services which covered the hundreds of miles between their current position and the capital.

"We were not expecting the CCF to have this fast-moving pursuit force pressuring us. They've prevented us from attacking the Chinese main line of support and slowing the divisions which are travelling along the route from Chamdo to Lhasa to our south-east. Instead, we've been reduced to fighting a series of defensive actions just to keep our units together."

Rhuzkoi nodded, "Da, but at least these tribesmen have not quarrelled and fought among themselves. I have been pleasantly surprised that they have maintained this military structure that they are so unaccustomed to ... and not reverted back to their disparate groups of regional clans of nomads. I have seen large formations such as this break down under pressure – like some of the Kazakh or Bashkir tribesmen who were conscripted into service in the Red Army."

"They all have one thing in common that keeps them united" advised Phuntsok. "Their devotion to the Dalai Llama."

Blackett looked at the Tibetan officer, noting how he spoke the name of their country's spiritual leader with a certain reverence. "Well … that is another thing we can be thankful for. Without it, this army would have disbanded by now and each tribe headed back to their own provinces to defend their homes."

He drew their attention back to the map, "Our original plans to disrupt the enemy rear are no longer viable under the current circumstances" he said. "We have to continue to stretch out the division that's been following us until they're forced to break off contact."

He moved his finger from their current position near Biru, still three hundred and fifty miles from Lhasa to their west, and down to the route being taken by the main CCF advance to the south-east.

"We've been gradually drawing our pursuers away from their main army but that means we will not be able to send out raiding parties against that main column because of the increasing distance between us and them."

He gave the other two a solemn look, "The division behind us'll be feeling the pinch from outrunning their supply lines, and we now have artillery, so we'll be in a position to engage that enemy force and hopefully inflict some heavier damage – maybe get them off our tail completely...but we aren't ready for that big fight yet. The casualties we cause them when they try to cross the river here will bolster our chances in any further battles against them."

Rhuzkoi looked at the map and then up at the Colonel, "But what about Lhasa? We will be allowing the main Chinese army to advance unhindered?"

"We can't afford to divide our force at this stage and try to slow them" answered Blackett. "If we send even a few companies of mounted soldiers we'll be weakening our situation here too much. We have to hope Lhasa will receive support from somewhere else."

Phuntsok, who had been listening quietly to one side, suddenly slapped his hands onto the map on the table, "No! We must stop them reaching Lhasa!" Tears welled up in his eyes as he pleaded to the foreigners for understanding. "Lhasa is everything! The Dalai Llama is there ... the Potala monastery – all that is most precious to our people is in that city!"

Blackett closed his eyes for a moment, then tried to console the Tibetan.

"We understand your distress. However, as you know we've been providing intelligence reports to our office, and we can be sure that the Union of Nations is being advised of the situation. We can only hope they decide to implement a Security Council resolution which will provide more substantial assistance."

"Da, Phuntsok my friend ... the Allies will come" added Rhuzkoi, "They will know what is happening here ... and they will come."

CHAPTER EIGHTEEN

*"I do conceive if the Army be not put into another method,
and the War more vigorously prosecuted, the People
can bear the war no longer, and will enforce
you to a dishonourable peace."*
Oliver Cromwell (to his fellow Roundheads)

UNASCOM HQ,
Dai-ichi Building
Tokyo,
Japan
April 29th, 1949

Major General Willoughby sipped his coffee thought-fully. He had been preparing for this meeting for weeks; gathering data and listening to the intelligence briefings from his G3 staff. Now he was pausing while the highest-ranking officers in the western hemisphere discussed one of his findings in depth.

Reports had been coming in for some time regarding the military materiel under production in China. It was obvious that the designs and prototypes had been obtained from the Soviets ... but from what source? Perhaps that question had just been answered.

That morning, as he was making the final preparations for the meeting, a verification had arrived. A report that had confirmed the rumours to be true – Stalin was alive.

The two five-star generals, MacArthur and Patton, to-gether with Major General William Chase, the Third Army

Chief of Staff, talked animatedly about the potential repercussions from Stalin's reappearance.

"George ..." said MacArthur sternly. He had warmed considerably to his senior field commander in the weeks they had spent working together, so they spoke freely to each other at all times. "I agree this may complicate the immediate plans for Operation Freehand, but Stalin's presence in the Russian Far East will only have a minimal impact on the entire Asia-Pacific conflict."

"Yes Douglas," Patton conceded, "... but we need to consider what effect it may have on the morale of the Soviet soldiers in the short term. All of a sudden, they have a figurehead for their cause. They're no longer a mere puppet of the Chinese communists – their propaganda machine will harp on about the old days of their so-called 'Great Patriotic War' against the Nazis ... evoking memories in those Red Army troops who'd fought and won against them. They'll have a reinforced belief that they are fighting to regain their homeland!"

"Stalin might also invoke memories of the Red Army's crushing defeats," replied MacArthur. "Both at the hands of the Allies, and from Vlasov's Russian Liberation Army when they matched into Moscow."

Sitting at the head of the long table in the centre of the conference room, MacArthur leaned his towering frame forward to emphasise his words. "The Soviets will be bolstered ... I agree – but the free Russians could also respond favourably to this news. We expect to hear from President Vlasov later today," he said as he looked at Willoughby, who gave him an affirmative nod.

MacArthur continued, "A more concerted effort from the Russian Army in the north will force the communists to continue to divert resources away from their units defending the eastern coast and Vladivostok. This opens the door for us to consider a large-scale amphibious operation on the Russian east coast instead of moving UoN forces into the region using the Trans-Siberian railway."

Willoughby interjected, "The Russian Republic will still need more military support from the Union of Nations. Their economy is struggling to recover from the destruction caused by the retreating Red Army at the end of the last war."

MacArthur gave his assent, "I'll be advising Washington of such. The administration should be taking more notice of my recommendations in light of the developments around Stalin, and hopefully they will pressure the UoN for more aid to the Russians."

Patton became annoyed at the mention of politics, "Blast those pathetic sycophants in Washington! They're more concerned with retaining office than winning a war." He got out of his seat and growled, "I'm going to be sending hundreds of thousands of men into extremely difficult terrain, and now Stalin's back it'll be against an even more desperate enemy!"

As he strode past Willoughby and up to the large wall map of the Far Eastern theatre, he pointed to the front lines of the Russian/Soviet conflict to the north of Vladivostok, "Here, around Khabarovsk where the Soviets have pushed Vlasov's forces back once again ... and further to the south in the Primorsky Krai region ... the rivers, swamps, dense taiga forest and highlands – are all more suited to the entrenched defender."

He moved his baton across the border to the west and into China. "It's not until we retaliate directly against the Chinese communists and push into their territory that we'll have widespread terrain favourable to our armour."

MacArthur joined Patton at the wall, putting his hands on his waist and studying the region carefully for a moment. He could see what Patton was saying. The expected battles following any possible landings in Far East Russia would, in the face of potentially stiffer opposition resulting from Stalin's presence, now need to be given further thought. The composition of the units involved in the landings would need to be configured accordingly. He asked Willoughby to set up a meeting with the overall commander of the combined landing forces, Admiral Barbey.

After making a note, Willoughby finished his coffee and then took advantage of the pause in proceedings to move back to the pedestal and resume his briefing.

"With respect sirs ... I'd like to add some detail to General MacArthur's opinion with regard to the overall strategic situation."

Patton and MacArthur returned to their seats.

"I think we all agree the resolve of the Soviets will be strengthened," said the Intelligence Chief. "We're talking about their most hardline divisions ... former NKVD battalions – the ones who used to follow up behind the Red Army units and machine gun anyone who tried to avoid the fighting. These are the same Russian communists who rounded up hundreds of thousands of their own people and those of neighbouring countries and inflicted a virtual death sentence by putting them into forced labour camps and the gulags."

Willoughby breathed out heavily. Compiling his research during the previous weeks had disturbed him greatly. Almost all the information had been suppressed by the Soviets and only been made available by Vlasov's Russian Republic after Moscow had been liberated. Together with the more recent reports of atrocities coming out of communist China, it painted a very harrowing picture – even for a seasoned veteran of many years of war. Now Willoughby's distress was showing as he tried to convey the nature of the communist enemy that would be facing the troops of the commanders sitting before him.

"It was the Soviets who set the standard for the Nazis. They exterminated Jews in their pogroms and shunted trainloads of the victims of their great socialist experiment off to death camps, systematically eliminating the elements of society they deemed to be a threat to communism – decades before Hitler used the same methods in the Holocaust."

Willoughby had everyone's attention. He let out a sad and ironical chuckle, "And frankly gentlemen ... now the Chinese are making the Bolsheviks look like amateurs."

MacArthur raised his eyebrows. He knew his G3 wasn't prone to exaggeration. The information he'd received from his sources behind the 'bamboo curtain' had clearly upset him.

Willoughby continued gravely, "Stalin may have been responsible for the deaths by starvation of several millions when he enforced collectivism in the Soviet Union, but the death toll from Mao's program in China *is going to be ten times worse than that.*"

Patton scowled and shook his head, "What is it with these goddammed backward countries! Don't they know what it is to be a human being anymore?"

The old warhorse, a soldier who'd seen more bloodshed in three world wars than any of his contempories would care to remember, sagged back into his chair. "Murdering millions of their own people," he lamented, "... and turning those people into lemmings who fight wars to prop up the very state that is torturing and oppressing them!"

Willoughby allowed a few moments for the air to clear after Patton's outburst, then added, "I'm afraid I can't provide a clearer picture than that," he said with some difficulty.

He picked up a sheaf of papers that had also been distributed to those in attendance. "My report will show that once Stalin and the Soviets have been dealt with, we can expect massive casualties on all fronts in a ground war with the Chinese."

CHAPTER NINETEEN

Chinese Communist Party (CCP) House of Reception,
Peking
April 30th, 1949

Josef Stalin was feeling once again like he was the Boss. Beneath his worsted serge tunic covered with medals, his chest brimmed with pride. He glared at the aide walking beside him, who immediately slowed his pace and fell into step one yard astern.

Stalin had been waiting three years for this day, biding his time while hiding in exile as a guest of the Chinese. After the recent successes of the Soviet army against the Russian Republic in the Russian Far East, the Bolsheviks were strong enough for him to finally show his hand, and the Soviets had now proclaimed his reinstatement at their head.

He glanced back at his aide again to check he was a sufficient distance behind him. When he walked through the twin doors looming up ahead at the end of the corridor, he wanted to be a solitary figure – symbolic of the isolated situation of his fellow Bolsheviks in Vladivostok. *Isolated yes ... but we will soon not be so alone.*

Although he remained unsmiling as was his custom, thoughts of the forthcoming reception brought forth a wave of goodwill for his Chinese hosts. He cast his mind back to the day three years before, when he had walked through another set of doors to meet with the leadership of the fledgling CCP. The designs and prototypes he'd provided them with had changed the course of their civil war, and resulted in the abrupt defeat of the Nationalists and their exile to the island of Taiwan. Stalin thought gleefully of the gift he carried with him this time, securely locked away in the briefcase he was carrying.

The ornate doors swung open. The House of Reception within Peking's Forbidden City was a former residence of those who had held imperial power down through the centuries. The palatial surroundings, although distinctly oriental in style, reminded Stalin of some the palaces in the former Soviet Union that had also been confiscated from a deposed nobility. *And now the CCP demonstrate the same level of power from within the same palaces.*

Once Stalin had made his entrance and stood pompously just inside the doorway, a CCP official announced, "His Excellency, Josef Stalin – Prime Minister of the Far Eastern Soviet."

Flash bulbs from the cameras of the international press blazed, accompanied by an incessant but restrained applause from the assembled Party dignitaries. Stalin walked straight up to the dais where for the first time he publicly shook hands with his protector, Chairman Mao Zedong.

The reception lasted for an hour and included an announcement that Mao's China would now recognise the Far Eastern Soviet as the legitimate state of Russia, and that he would pledge his government's support for their cause. Several speeches were given by higher ranking Party officials, such as the recently promoted Prime Minister Zhou Enlai, all of which were made as though Stalin were setting foot in their country for the first time. Only a select few within the CCP knew that the man they were receiving into their midst had been sheltering incognito in Peking for the years since his 'mistaken' death in an air crash. The official explanation for his absence was that Stalin had been recovering from injuries incurred while relocating the Soviet capital from Moscow to Vladivostok.

Mao signalled an end to the proceedings, and he took Stalin, along with Zhou, to a nearby anteroom.

In the secluded confines of the meeting room, Mao spoke frankly through an interpreter. "Now that you have made your reappearance there will be much concern from the western powers."

As he spoke, he smoothed a few of the wrinkles in his drab grey suit, as though exemplifying he was in the process of straightening out more than just his attire. "The Union of Nations has approved a resolution to assist the Russian Republic and put an end to your civil war. We have so far provided you with much in the way of military ordnance, but I think it is time to reflect further on the future expectations of your struggle."

Stalin responded patiently, "Your comrades in Russia are grateful for everything you have done for them as they fight to save the People's Revolution."

He sat across from Mao on the opposite side of a long wooden table, his ample frame appeared to recline comfortably although the uncushioned chairs were stark and rigid, and he was making it look as though he were in control of proceedings. "We will continue to seek your material support … perhaps with an additional assurance that your Peoples Liberation Army will intervene should the western imperialists become involved and encroach on the borders of Soviet territory."

Mao scoffed, "Comrade Stalin, we have already committed the bulk of our armies to the defence of our own borders. Those same western imperialists have initiated a war against our revolution by invading our Korean neighbours. They also continue their colonial expansion into Indo-china from where we are sure they intend to launch an invasion of our country."

Mao took off his plain peaked cap which matched his suit by its dullness and planted it onto the table in frustration. "The Kuomintang nationalists also threaten to invade the mainland from Taiwan with the support of the Americans. How do you propose we defend against all of these attacks and still send troops into your country?"

Stalin had something in mind, but he was biding his time in an effort to draw Mao out further and strengthen his negotiating position. He continued to sit back quietly, holding a blank expression.

Mao grew more agitated, "From your silence I can see that we are correct in our assessment. President Vlasov will most certainly brand you as a war criminal and will resolve himself to bring you to justice. We would be better accommodated by distancing ourselves from your conflict."

He pushed his cap further to one side, giving himself more room in front of him to point accusingly with his finger. "Your failed struggle is an embarrassment to our own victorious socialist revolution!" he spat vehemently. "Why should we send our peasants to die in a futile attempt at what would appear to be a forlorn hope?"

Stalin was unmoved. He let slip an almost invisible smirk, and then leaned forward clasping his chubby hands together on the table. "It is true that my former countrymen have considered me to be a criminal ... albeit posthumously until now. You should take heed of that! And treat it as a warning of how the West will also view your venerable self in time."

He grew dark and serious as he looked directly at the Chinese Chairman, "You are going to assist us in any way you can because I have once again brought you something that will ensure your hold on power, and the success of both our revolutions."

Mao lost his remaining poise as the two leaders stared each other down. His iron jaw slackened in the face of Stalin's even more arrogant stance, and the Chinese leader's eyes narrowed as he returned the Russian's smug glare. He watched angrily as the Bolshevik Prime Minister motioned to his aide who hurriedly placed a briefcase on the table. Stalin opened it and slid the contents across to Zhou.

The Prime Minister looked carefully through the documents with a confused expression on his face. Stalin spread out his hands, "Comrade ... you were perhaps expecting more blueprints – a more advanced fighter jet, or the designs for the V2 rockets we captured from the Nazis?"

Mao looked at Zhou questioningly, but only received a shrug in response.

Stalin chuckled softly, revelling in their discomfort. He'd been hiding among them for years and deeply resented the condescension and contempt he'd received from Mao and his Party members.

"There are many communist sympathisers throughout the so-called 'free world' – some of whom have taken it upon themselves to obtain for us the one significant item that gives the imperialists their power. I bring you the means of dissolving that power and holding the world to ransom ... the plans for building an atomic bomb!"

CHAPTER TWENTY

"For many are the trees of God that grow
In Paradise, and various, yet unknown
To us, in such abundance lies our choice,
As leaves a greater store of fruit untouched,
Still hanging incorruptible, till men
Grow up to their provision, and more hands
Help to disburden nature of her birth."
John Milton
Paradise Lost

Mojave City
2268 CE

A fountain's trickle spoke of the renewal of life's essence to Eya's garden. She listened, as did the floral audience in her care.

She moved from flower to sapling, aged bough to emerging shoot, and dispensed the skill of her craft for their benefit. She breathed in the flowers' intoxicating scent and felt at one with the lifeforce of her plants, and with the hope of a perpetual spring.

A new arrival to her garden, a small tree with broad fingered leaves, called her to attend. She stepped closer to examine the bright green profusion at the end of one of the branches.

"Arjon! Come look at this!"

Arjon, hearing the joy in her voice, left his work in the den and hurried across the atrium.

"What is it?" he asked. "Have some of the seeds from the Spire germinated?"

"It's the young tree they asked me to look after. Here! It's budding!"

Arjon stepped carefully through a bed of annuals and peered at eye level to the lowest branch. The new growth was glowing with a bright luminosity, and the impression it gave Arjon was that of a forthcoming gift.

"Why, I've never seen anything like this" he said with amazement. "What tree is it?"

"The Spire entrusted it to me as part of a new research project. Only a select few of us were chosen to be caretakers" she said with pride. "The species has been responding best to close personal attention, rather than a laboratory environment."

"And so ... what will the fruit be like?"

"That's what's so special about it ... it's called *arborvitae nutrensis.*"

The rudimentary Latin Arjon had picked up from his legal background gave him a rough translation, "Tree of Life's Nutrients ... so the fruit must be good for you?"

"It's more than just good" Eya corrected him as she brushed her fingers lightly over the velvety buds, "The fruit contains the complete spectrum of carbohydrates, vitamins and minerals ... and even proteins, that are thought to be optimal for human nutrition."

"All of them? That's fantastic!"

"And eating the fruit is different to just taking those nutrients as a supplement – the bioavailability is the key."

Her hand cupped a single budding stem, and Arjon thought he saw a response to Eya's touch from the plant.

"The Spire of Evolution believe that as we humans evolve, we influence and shape the other components of life on Earth – so we grow in unison."

"Ah ... I see. And do they think that you may be able to help this tree evolve – and that your care will influence the ability of the fruit to be more ... *compatible* with humans?"

"Basically yes. Think of the process of domestication of animals such as horses or dogs ... or the collaboration between plants and their pollinators. One theory of evolution places the logic for such relationships as being due to a random process of trial and error – or natural selection. The Spire think there are many exceptions to that theory, and I expect the 'Influencer' idea may have been developed further as a result of the Enlightenment of the Soul."

Arjon thought at once how the Enlightenment of 2265 had changed their world in so many ways. The idea of the human spirit interacting with that of other life forms made perfect sense.

Plants had been thought to possess a spirit, or lifeforce, long before the Enlightenment proved that one existed for humans. One of the experiments demonstrated in the Enlightenment's presentation had shown the ghostly outline of a leaf remaining after it had been cut from the live plant. It followed that if there is some kind of underlying life-force – then communication between the host entities may be possible.

Arjon mused once again on the Enlightenment's implications, sharing his speculation with his wife, "We have so many more questions about the soul. It's possibly eternal ... and most certainly existing across multiple lifetimes. What does it mean? Are we ever really *young*? Or old? Is age in years a redundant concept? Is there such a thing as a virgin, or a truly innocent babe? How much of our previous lives do we carry with us into our next host? Does this explain why our personalities may be completely unexpected considering our upbringing ... why a child may be given every opportunity and encouragement to become a good person by their genetics and environment combined – but still turn out to be bad?"

Eya put a comforting hand on top of his. "Sweetheart ... the answers to those questions may one day come to light, but for now – one thing is absolutely true for all of us: to deny the existence of one's soul – is to deny oneself an afterlife."

Arjon smiled at her, looked at the tree and then sighed, *Qwerty, I need multiple lifetimes just to think about all the possibilities.*

The tree with its glimmering buds returned his thoughts to that which they'd been considering before being sidetracked. Eya's work was not intended to provide anything more than 'proof by example' of the tree evolving so that its adaptations enabled it to produce a fruit whose qualities were ideally suited for humans.

He asked her, "As a kind of experiment, could the fruit be developed in another way? Would a laboratory-raised tree, or even its seeds, selectively bred for the same purpose – with no human contact or even possible *awareness* of humans – achieve the same results that you are hoping for?"

Eya became excited, "I know that my little tree, living here in complete harmony among our floral family, is going to outperform anything grown in some impersonal or robotic mass production facility!"

Arjon kissed her, "You're amazing! Let's go out an celebrate!"

"Wonderful idea! But don't you have some work to do?"

Arjon thought with frustration at how even their part-time assignments tended to interfere with the more important aspects of their lives, such as socialising. "Yes ... but it won't take me very long," he said determinedly. Then he called out to the bower, "Hesta, make a reservation for this evening for dinner."

"And invite Margeaux and Grillon!" added Eya.

Arjon returned to his den and picked up where he'd left off. He'd been arranging to meet with a contact from the Directory of Purpose, Coralex, who would be reviewing the progress of the development of Hesta's latest simulation. He donned the Immerser and felt a tingle as the electro-sensitive conductors made an active connection to his cerebral cortex.

Opening his eyes, he found himself standing below a snow-capped mountain. A snake-like thread of blue wound its way through the Yarlung Tsung River valley far below. He knew where he was; Lhoka, the rebel stronghold two hundred kilometres south of Lhasa. This was the Tibet of the alternative world – a history so unlike his own, yet it also contained many similar events. Here, there was no Union of Nations intervening in the Chinese invasion. Here, Jizhu Geist was also fighting for freedom ... but the outcome would be very different.

He started walking along a trail leading to where he'd arranged to meet Coralex. The trail led to a large structure built on top of a rocky spur. The white walls of its multiple tiers which followed the slope upwards were topped by the ceramic tiled spires typical of the Tibetan monasteries. Arjon went through the gates at the ground level and entered a large courtyard. A woman sitting at a table beneath a flowering tree waved to him, and he walked over to join her.

"Welcome to Lhoka!" she said cheerfully, "So nice to finally meet you in person!"

Arjon laughed as he took her hand, "And you! But it feels more like in spirit than in person."

"Your AI has done an amazing job with this simulation – that Dzo beside the trail on the way here was spectacular!"

"Oh … you mean that cross between a long-haired yak and a cow?" Arjon replied, "I read that their condensed milk is a delicacy."

The Immerser was doing its job of providing the visitors with the background information they needed so they could blend into their new environment and become an active part of the simulation.

"Your tunic is very impressive" she observed. "Is that silk?"

Arjon noticed he was wearing a straight cut blue sherwani with an intricate geometric pattern down the front. He also saw that Coralex's dress was a simple saree with a matching silk sash draped across her shoulder.

"Silk … yes. It makes sense for us to look like visitors from India doesn't it?"

A monk brought them an ornate pot full of tea, and Arjon asked him if he knew the whereabouts of the man they'd come to meet. The monk nodded and walked serenely back through the inner monastery's wooden doors to find Ji-zhu.

Coralex wondered at their ancient surroundings. The walls overgrown by flowering vines and the beautifully tended garden in which they sat imparted a tranquil sense of peace and wisdom. "What do you expect to find here?" she asked.

"Missing pieces" said Arjon. "We know a lot about Ji-zhu's later life, how he helped shape our world and influenced the creation of the Pillars ... but we know little about his earlier years."

"So, you are hoping this simulation will provide some insight?"

"More than that. Hesta has shown how these probability matrices can accurately demonstrate not just the events and their causes in an alternative world, but also the thought processes and personalities of the people involved in those events."

"I see. Then we can expect a simulated Ji-zhu to be able to describe his childhood ... and his years thereafter?"

"In detail." Arjon was enthralled by the possibilities. "Imagine it! We are about to meet one of the founders of our civilisation!"

"Yes ... albeit in an artificially generated alternative reality," Coralex pointed out with some reservation as she scrutinised her surroundings more thoroughly.

To Arjon, Coralex had at first seemed enthusiastic, but now he thought she'd begun to hold back somewhat. He assumed it was because she was a representative of the Directory of Purpose. *Probably because this investigation would be critical to her career,* he thought. *Being an outside contractor, I guess I'm under less pressure and can keep all of this at arm's length...but I'm still excited that I'm about to meet a legend from the past!*

He leant across the table to whisper in case any of the monks were in earshot, "Are you also able to recall the details of the crisis here in Tibet? And the overall situation with the rest of the world?"

Coralex sipped from her teacup, and considered for a moment, then nodded affirmatively, "I think so ... the communists have invaded, and the Tibetan's are helpless to try and stop them. The so-called 'United Nations' have ignored the country's pleas for assistance and the Chinese Army has now occupied Lhasa."

Arjon saw that she was having difficulty processing her emotions. She frowned and a confused look appeared on her face. *Perhaps I'm not as exposed to the discomfort as she is because I've done this before,* he thought. He put a hand on her arm, "It's okay ... I know none of this makes sense right now ... just keep a part of your mind free to remember that we'll be leaving here before too long."

After a moment, she gave him a more confident and grateful glance. "Thank you, that has helped."

"You're welcome, but also remember that we must be mindful of Ji-zhu's predicament. The Chinese are brutally exterminating the Tibetan people and destroying their culture. Here in the mountains around Lhoka, the Khampa rebels are fighting a losing battle to stem the invasion. All they can do now is try to hold them up so that the small Tibetan column escorting the Dalai Llama south into India can make their escape."

Coralex nodded as her mind tried to reconcile her conflicting memories. She was aware that in her own world Ji-zhu had fought alongside the Tibetan Army and the Khampas who had been supported by an international force of mostly American military advisors at the auspices of the Union of Nations. Here in the simulation, there was no such support, and the depleted Khampa rebels had dispersed and retreated into the mountains south-east of Lhasa where they were trying to delay the Chinese and cover the Dalai Llama's escape across the mountains into India.

The doors opened and a man wearing a sheepskin vest and leathers walked over to them. "My friends ... I am thankful that you are here."

As Ji-zhu sat down next to them, Arjon thought he looked as out of place among the crimson-robed monks as he and Coralex did.

"Ji-zhu ..." Arjon took a breath, straining to hold his composure, but then Hesta strengthened the Immerser's synaptic bonding and 'reminded' him of the purpose of the meeting. "... we have heard of your country's plight and would like to hear more about what is happening here."

Ji-zhu looked weary. The months spent surviving in the mountains had taken their toll. His eyes narrowed, "What is happening here is genocide – plain and simple."

As though his words had given him strength and a re-newed resolve, he added, "I have come to this monastery to try to convince the High Llama that they should leave. The Chinese will be here soon and will destroy this place and murder anyone in it."

Coralex gasped with outrage, "But why? It's so peaceful here ... why would anyone wish to harm these people?"

"Why?" Ji-zhu demanded, "Because the communists are demonstrating to the Tibetans that their religion is a form of weakness. By committing atrocities against the monks and the nuns, by systematically plundering and then demol-ishing the monasteries ... they are showing these people that they are helpless – and that their spiritual beliefs can-not help them."

Ji-zhu's inner turmoil showed that he felt his words were failing to do justice to the brutality and crimes against hu-manity occurring all around him.

"What about the Khampas?" asked Arjon, "How long can they hold out here?"

"They are very tough ... but against modern weapons, planes and artillery they can do little. I see this war will end before long, and that Tibet as we know it will disappear."

Coralex was deeply affected by his sorrow and despair. "This is terrible. Is there anything we can do?"

"You can go back and tell the rest of the world what has happened here. Nothing more."

Arjon could see a fire burning inside Ji-zhu – one that spoke of never giving up on his fight against the communists and their criminal culture as they invaded his country.

"And you?" asked Arjon, "You don't seem to be the same as the other rebels. What is *your* story?"

Ji-zhu shrugged at the question, "Yes I expect I am not the same ... but I am still a Tibetan – just one who has seen more of this world and what lies beyond it than many other people."

Arjon's expression begged for the man, who in an alternative life would do so much for the world, to continue. "What *does* lie beyond it? Are you also a monk?"

"No. I do not follow any specific religion, but I have seen that it can have a positive impact on those who seek spiritual nourishment."

"If you please ... tell us more about yourself" asked Arjon.

Ji-zhu had relaxed to these foreigners somewhat after being able to unburden himself upon them. He smiled knowingly, "Do you think that you possess the ears to hear?"

The Tibetan sat back and considered his visitors from India, recalling the journey in search of answers that he'd taken years before to that mystical land. "I sense within both of you, that you are aware you have a soul. What does that mean to you?"

Coralex responded immediately, as though it were a question she had asked herself recently and already had an answer prepared, "It means that I will live again."

Arjon looked at her, "You have obviously given that question some thought before" he said, finding that although he'd worked on cases for clients seeking compensation for losses incurred from their disconnection to the past lives of their souls, he hadn't given serious thought to the future – or the future of his own soul.

Ji-zhu reached across and took Coralex's hand. As her face lit up at the contact, Arjon suddenly noticed how pretty she looked.

The Tibetan spoke to her in a deep, convincing tone, "You have no fear of death, do you?"

Coralex hesitated, but realised he was right. "No ... I suppose I don't." After thinking for a moment, she added, "I expect I'm more concerned with fearing that I may have led a wasted life. It's what drives me...compels me to improve myself and become a better person."

Ji-zhu released her hand and smiled warmly, "Then I hope your courage continues to lead you to search for more than you already know."

Coralex nodded, "Yes, I'm sure that I will." She bowed her head slightly, looking down at her hands, "I intend to find out more about reincarnation, and its significance to your culture."

Arjon was encouraged by what he was seeing of the agent from the Directory of Purpose. Obviously, she had been selected for this assignment for a reason.

Ji-zhu's penetrating gaze fixed on Arjon. The utopian felt he was on the cusp of receiving something very special, but that it was something he may not be worthy of receiving.

"Friend, there is so much we do not know. About the entirety of our spirit, the nature of the universe and how we interact with it. I have been fortunate to have found some answers to that which I did not even know the questions."

Again, that disarming smile conveyed compassion and made Arjon feel a sense of mutual goodwill.

Ji-zhu continued, "Earlier you asked about my life. I expect the place for me to begin is where I was shown where it all *ends*."

He closed his eyes in contemplation for a few moments, then reopened them slowly before continuing, "In a vision I was shown the end of the universe. The experience left me searching intently for insights into why such an event must occur."

"You saw *our* universe...end?" asked Coralex.

"Yes. I was shown by God. Importantly, the question I was left asking myself was, *why* does it not continue for eternity? There are also ramifications from a Buddhist perspective ... does this also mean we cannot seek eternal life after our many reincarnations? If we acknowledge that we have a soul, then eventually we should question the nature of its existence when it is not linked to a human body. If our souls are connected to this reality for a purpose, such as becoming spiritually enlightened, then what are the consequences for those who do not achieve such enlightenment? I had wished to return to India to further investigate Hindu scriptures and see if they can shed any light on this but the situation here in Tibet has prevented it."

The two utopians were entranced by the mystic's words. It was as if he were speaking directly to their inner spirit and bypassing their logical and instinctively reluctant minds.

Coralex stirred and gathered her thoughts sufficiently enough to respond, "I've also asked myself many questions about my soul" she explained. "In the society to which we belong, we have proven that it exists!", she added with dignified enthusiasm. "We have a mantra … *Who you were, who you are, who you will be.*"

She could see that as a Buddhist, Ji-zhu understood that the mantra did not refer to 'who you were' before some significant change of character or behaviour in the context of a person's current life – it literally meant who you were in a previous life or lives lived by your soul.

"It is hoped that the mantra, and our society's newly enlightened purpose will help us to ascend from a more material past and assist us to evolve toward a more perfect future."

Ji-zhu look pleased, and Coralex was delighted with herself that she could relate on such a level to one of the founders of the Pillars.

She added, "It's the 'who you will be' part that interests me the most. We have heard about your wisdom from many other Tibetans … is there anything you might be able to share with us about incarnation and the expectations for our future lives?"

"Only that you need to seek the truth. Enlightenment is universal, and if you are fortunate enough to receive guidance you should accept it with an open mind. Too many people choose to reject what they do not immediately understand … which can lead them to become defensive or hostile. This may lead to ignorance, or worse, intolerance."

He sipped his tea reverently, as though it were a luxury to which he'd been deprived while up in the cold and rugged mountains. He continued, "The Buddhists live their lives mindful that they will live again in the future. This awareness of living multiple lives according to karmic principles teaches us many virtues, such as patience, thankfulness and humility. It also means we can live our lives with a heightened sense of purpose. We will be accountable for our actions in this life, and so 'who you will be' will be determined by how well we live *this* life."

Hesta sensed that Arjon and Coralex were reaching the limit of their virtual endurance and gave them a gentle nudge that it was time to end the session. Arjon spoke politely to Ji-zhu, "We must go now, but we would like to call on you again in the future."

The Tibetan nodded and went back inside the monastery.

As the synaptic connections to their Immersers began to weaken, Arjon said to Coralex, "I'd like to speak to you in person once we return."

"Certainly. We can discuss what we've learned here, and I'll explain more about my role at the Directory."

"Fine" said Arjon, "I'd also like to invite my contact from the Centre of Truth – if you have no objections?"

"The CoT? My, you do move in high circles ... of course. I'm looking forward to it."

His perception blurred and then Arjon became aware that he was back in his den. He placed his headset to one side and Eya walked in.

She laced her hand softly on his brow, "Do you need to recover after that? We can celebrate my assignment to the Spire some other time."

"No, no ... I'm ok. There was less of the harrowing and more of the illuminating with that session. I just need to dictate some notes to Hesta and then I'll get ready."

Eya left to get dressed, leaving Arjon deep in thought about his research into Ji-zhu's past. He knew that any mention of God was going to complicate his findings.

We may have proven the soul exists ... but God is another matter entirely.

Then he thought of Coralex. He felt reassured that anything of a spiritual nature that he reported would be confirmed by her. He sighed with relief that he would be working with such an enlightened soul. He asked Hesta to schedule a meeting and to also invite Thiessen.

CHAPTER TWENTY-ONE

Gyalmo Ngulchu River,
South-west Kham Province,
Eastern Tibet
June 6th, 1949

As he rounded a turn on the narrow mountainside trail, Lieutenant Phuntsok could see the white-watered green streak of the fast-flowing Gyalmo Ngulchu far below. The trail had been following the river and winding its way between sparse trees and boulders deposited just beneath the snowline, since they'd left camp the previous day. As he stepped off the dry, dusty track to allow a pack horse to pass by him, he had to reach for a handhold on a big boulder so he could keep his balance on the steep incline.

Although two funnels of steam puffed downwards from the horse's nostrils courtesy of the chilled mountain air, the animal didn't appear to be labouring under its load. Phuntsok marvelled at the stamina and toughness of the Riwoche, a breed native to the Kham region, and the most important part of its Khampa handler's life apart from his rifle.

After taking a swig from his canteen to help clear his altitude-induced headache, his breath soon recovered and Phuntsok stepped back in line and resumed the march around the peak. Continuing behind and below him, the supply train stretched for hundreds of yards before disappearing into the forested tree-line and out of sight. Ahead, the path gained another several hundred feet of elevation before reaching the next switchback. That was the point where they would leave the trail and follow a goat track to their destination, a small plateau overlooking the river.

Lobsang jogged up beside him, leading his own horse and carrying a Lee-Enfield rifle over his shoulder. A gift from the British Army to his father, the rifle had been passed down to him many years before.

"Not more far brother," the chieftain advised him in his broken English which had improved in the previous weeks. The chieftain knew that Phuntsok, a native of the lower altitudes of Lhasa, was taking some time to acclimate to the thinner air of the high mountains.

As Lobsang continued past, Phuntsok noticed the two bandoliers brimming with .303 cartridges criss-crossed over the back of the Khampa's sheepskin coat, reminding him that there was no shortage of that high-calibre ammunition, as it was regularly traded from the caravans travelling through Tibet from northern India.

Behind Lobsang, also moving along effortlessly and leading his horse by the reins, followed Ji-zhu. The Teacher slowed and spoke quietly, "The men are ready for this fight Phuntsok. Lead them as though they were the same as those men in your regular army – they will not let you down."

Ji-zhu patted the M1 Garand slung by his side, "With our new weapons we will give cause for the communists to rethink their plans for taking us on in *our* mountains."

He moved on, leaving Phuntsok to consider the most unusual of the guerrilla leaders. Ji-zhu had told them what he'd seen when he'd travelled through Xinjiang province, the region of north-western China, formerly known as East-Turkistan, and inhabited by the Uighur, Kazakh and Kirghiz peoples. They too were being terrorised by communist Chinese invaders, and tens of thousands were being sent to concentration camps for 're-education'. As a result, Ji-zhu had already despised communism and the corrupting influence its ideology had on people, well before the Tibetan invasion.

With the effects of rehydration taking hold, Phuntsok's pace quickened, and he walked on, brushing his way past some of the slower-moving horses carrying the heavier loads of artillery pieces that had been received from the recent airdrops. He shifted his rifle to his other shoulder. It was also one of the American M1s, the training for which the Khampas had been receiving since the resupply by air. Blackett and Rhuzkoi were both still conducting the weapons handling classes back at the main camp. That, plus the ongoing issues such as language differences when issuing urgent commands, and problems with them adjusting to the higher altitudes, had forced the decision for the two foreigners to remain back at headquarters instead of joining this reconnaissance in force.

The weapons training would soon be completed however, as the senior Khampas, once they had received their own training with machine guns, rifles and grenades, were then passing on their knowledge to the thousands of guerrillas under their respective command.

Knowing both of the CIG field operatives very well after spending the previous winter months quartered with them in Chamdo, Phuntsok wondered how long it would be before Blackett and Rhuzkoi rejoined the fighting.

Not long from the way they were climbing up the walls of my house impatiently waiting for the inevitable invasion to begin.

It struck him how strange it was that they had seemed so certain that the communist encroachment into Tibet was a foregone conclusion. *Almost as if they had privileged information that it was going to happen.*

His ponderings returned to the immediate situation. As he neared the exit point to the goat track, he started to go through the upcoming procedures he would need to follow once they arrived at the plateau. After Colonel Blackett had finishing instructing him in the use and deployment of the 75mm pack howitzers, he had been given overall command of this mission. As he walked alongside a Riwoche carrying a barrel section and some wooden boxes of the high-explosive ammunition for one of the howitzers, he visualised how he would be deploying his artillery for the impending battle.

In an effort to outflank the Tibetan rebel army, the pursuing CCF division had started construction of a timber bridge six miles downstream from the main guerrilla positions. Khampa scouts had soon discovered the site, and now Phuntsok had to determine how his column was going to destroy it.

The Chinese had recognised the type of artillery the rebels had started using against them, and as they had previously acquired some of the same type of US mountain guns from the defeated Kuomintang Nationalists during the civil war, they knew its effective range. Consequently, they were building their bridge just beyond the five and half mile limit of the howitzers.

Four of the howitzers had been assigned for the job, and once in position, Phuntsok thought he would need to lay down a barrage on to the opposite bank. As the terrain on either side of the crossing was very steep, he would need to site the guns with a direct line of fire onto the bridge, as their rounds couldn't be brought to bear from a distance due to the howitzers' limited elevation of forty-five degrees.

As he ran through the process in his mind, he knew they'd have to try to remain undetected for as long as possible – at least until the guns had been unloaded and reassembled, or else risk prematurely coming under fire from the communists. He looked up at the sky. *Still a few hours of daylight left. We should be able to deploy the guns and then be ready to launch the attack tomorrow at dawn.*

As the trail reached the next switchback, he noticed that the elderly Khampa in charge of the pack horse he'd been following was looking fatigued. Phuntsok took the lead rope from his withered hand and beckoned for him to rest by the side of the track. The Tibetan Army officer then led the horse onto the goat track and continued along the thin path beaten bare over the centuries by Himalayan Blue sheep. As it followed the natural contour of the steep slope, it offered a panoramic view down to the distant stripe of the river several thousand feet below.

With no room to walk alongside, Phuntsok led his horse from the front as they carefully picked their way through the eroded rocks and rubble. They occasionally had to leave the path altogether at spots where the nimble sheep just leapt over obstacles such as small boulders or narrow streamlets washed away by the intense downpours that occurred below the snowline. At one such section, a deeply eroded channel caused Phuntsok to lead his horse up the slope, coaxing it forward and carefully placing its footfalls to avoid a fatal slip.

The rebel columns progress had slowed markedly on this rougher terrain, but after an hour, those at the front descended from the heights to the plateau overlooking the bridge. By the time Phuntsok joined them, dozens of foxholes were being dug. He handed the pack horse over to one of his men to be tied up along with the other horses who were tethered to a rope line strung across the back wall of the mile-long plateau, and out of sight of the ground far below. Then he gave orders for two of the howitzers which were already being assembled by their crews to be sited just back from the plateau's edge, where they could be moved forward to bring direct fire onto the bridge below.

Lobsang and Ji-zhu were laying down on the lip of the shelf, reconnoitring the river crossing below. Lobsang waved at Phuntsok to approach at a crawl.

Phuntsok walked to the edge and then dropped down to the ground with his rifle straddled across his outstretched arms. Once he'd sidled up beside the other two, he looked down to the bridge fifteen hundred feet below. His heart skipped a beat from the shocking realisation that the crudely assembled timber span was almost completed.

Extending for fifty feet from the completed sections of the bridge, he could see the river flowing beneath the pair of steel cables strung between the two banks to support the continuing construction. Chinese engineers swarmed about, carrying lengths of wood and laying them onto the supporting framework. They were ringed by tiny puffs of smoke as their accompanying guards returned sniper fire with a few rebels hidden in the trees on the riverbank below the plateau. As the shots echoed up and down the valley, the trio of rebel officers made their plans for the defence of the near-side bank.

"Some scouts been down there since yesterday. They try keep Chinese heads down" said Lobsang, using his English as much as possible to reinforce his learning.

"It looks like they might have given us the time we need ... from the look of it they may not be able to finish the bridge before tomorrow" replied Phuntsok.

He watched through his field glasses as one of the Chinese carrying one end of a length of timber was hit. His body toppled into the muddy-brown water and drifted away downstream. It took some time for the enemy to confirm the location of the source of the shot, but then a volley of return fire including several mortar rounds blasted out from the trees behind the bridge.

Phuntsok shifted his view to the forest lining the near bank and saw where the returning fire was directed. A series of flashes erupted among the treetops, targeting the sniper who had felled the engineer, and sending splintered branches and foliage flying into the smoke-filled air.

"I hope that sniper had time to change position like we trained him to," said Phuntsok.

Ji-zhu then pointed to a spot a hundred yards from where the salvo had landed. They could all see a pair of Khampas hurrying along in a crouch away from their former position. Ji-zhu smiled. His youthful face seemed to shine in unison with the sunlit landscape around him, "You have trained them well brother. We can rest assured the bridge will not be finished before the dawn."

As dusk closed quickly over the mountainside, Phuntsok deployed the remainder his artillery. In the dimness, the guns could be positioned without being observed by the enemy below. He placed a single gun several hundred yards away from the others with its sole purpose of destroying the bridge. It was expected that this gun's smoking discharge, once it had fired, would attract an immediate response from the enemy mortars below. The other guns he arranged spaced well apart from each other, with varying fields of fire in the expectation they would need to cover a broad area of forest concealing the communist positions on the opposite bank.

Meanwhile Lobsang and Ji-zhu organised the positioning of a platoon of mortars and the Khampa infantry. All the deployments were done quietly so that the Chinese below believed there were only a few Khampa snipers, and had no inkling that there were many more positioned with artillery on the plateau who were preparing to attack in the morning.

Darkness fell, and no campfires were allowed. The Khampas spent a cold night up on the heights, with only C-rations to sustain them.

At first light the following day, Phuntsok was roused from his bedroll by an urgent shaking. Consternation on the face of one of the night sentries told him something was wrong, and he scrambled out from under his blanket. All around, the waking rebels were rushing into position, and the lieutenant ran to the edge of the shelf. Far below, still hidden in the darkened shadows of the unrisen sun, Phuntsok strained to make out what was causing all the alarm. Then his eyes adjusted, revealing a huddle of Chinese engineers laying the last few timbers of the bridge. They'd worked through the night, and now the near bank was crawling with communist troops who had swum or waded the last remaining yards and were securing a beachhead.

Phuntsok raced over to the solitary gun where the crew was just finishing a check that the gunsights were lined up accurately on the bridge. The gun aimer called out "Identified!", and then Phuntsok shouted "Fire!"

The high-explosive round blasted out of the barrel and arced down towards the river. It landed in the water, sending a geyser fifty feet into the air beside the bridge.

Phuntsok saw the shot go wide through his glasses and watched as the troops who were gathering behind the engineers started to panic. Some of them jumped into the water, expecting another salvo to be imminent.

"Left 10 yards! Fire at will!"

Seconds later a second round of HE spat downwards, this time on target. The centre of the bridge disintegrated in a fiery balloon of shattered beams and flailing bodies.

The weakened structure immediately started breaking apart under the force of the current. The sections before and after the gaping hole in the centre broke off from the supporting cables and were carried away to be consumed by the pale green wash of the river.

Soldiers clambered over each other to get back to the far bank and escape the fast-dissolving bridge, but many were being swept away with the debris.

As the Tibetans had expected, the communist artillery below spotted the smoke discharge from the lone gun and soon responded. A few puffs of tell-tale smoke billowed from their positions hidden among the trees several hundred yards away across the river. Phuntsok shouted for the gun crew to take cover, and then dived into a ditch. Rocks, dirt and shrapnel flew above him as the resulting explosions shattered the lip of the shelf around the howitzer.

The rebel mortars and infantry began to fire on the Chinese troops who'd been waiting to cross, and were massed on the opposite bank. Phuntsok sprang up from cover and ran over to the other howitzer emplacements. Three heavy machine guns, one for each howitzer, opened up on the enemy artillery positions. Their tracer rounds would provide a continuous visual cue for the howitzers' gun aimers to direct their fire.

The enemy barrage, from Soviet designed ZiS-3 76mm field guns, continued until one salvo scored a direct hit on the howitzer that had destroyed the bridge. The howitzer's barrel spun through the air and struck the back wall of the plateau, narrowly missing the tied-up horses. A few broke loose from their ropes and galloped off in fright, pursued by their handlers.

The communist barrage ceased following the destruction of the gun, but now it was the turn of the remaining Khampa howitzers. They'd waited patiently holding their fire until the communist artillery had revealed their positions, and now Phuntsok heard the observer from the nearest crew calling out to his gun aimer, "Range eight hundred! HE! Target – artillery!"

The gun aimer responded, "Identified!"

"Fire!"

"On the way!" shouted the gunner.

The other howitzers also fired, and a trio of explosions expelled flame and smoke from the distant trees.

The observers called out corrections to each gun, "Up fifty! Zero one five degrees!"

Another volley boomed down from the plateau, and as the rolling echo faded away down the picturesque river valley, a huge fireball erupted from one of the targets.

"Hit!" cried the gun's observer.

Phuntsok moved his glasses across to the fireball, then saw a number of smaller explosions sending long tendrils of incandescence throughout the forest. He wondered for a moment, then realised it was the ammunition from one of the Chinese guns exploding.

A firefight ensued. Another battery of communist artillery joined the battle from five miles away. Their observers near the river zeroed them in on the gun flashes from the plateau and a dozen rounds curved their way through the light-blue sky toward their targets. Seconds later, explosions rocked the ground around Phuntsok, and when he popped his head up, he saw that the Khampas were taking many casualties.

Twenty yards away he saw a body, the bloody torso shredded by shrapnel and both legs missing. Cries from the wounded reached his ears above the sound and hurricane force concussions from more detonations. He ducked back down, shaking from terror, and burying his head beneath his arms. He shut his eyes hard to keep himself from panicking as the hot air pounded against his back. The spectre of Death was exhaling, laughing at him and taunting him to raise his head again – or else continue to cower in fear.

The incessant barrage from the ZiS-3s, each gun firing at over 15 rounds per minute, continued unabated. As he forced himself to quell his fears, Phuntsok found the courage to act. Seeing that the rebels were being outgunned, Phuntsok rose unsteadily to his feet and ordered a withdrawal, "Move the guns!" he shouted.

The order was relayed along the edge of the plateau, and the gun crews ran from their slit trenches and worked feverishly to push their guns back from the lip of the shelf. Phuntsok knew it was more important to keep them for another fight on another day, rather than lose any of them in this one. They were quickly hitched to waiting harness horses and towed away.

The fire rate of the Chinese guns gradually fell away to conserve ammunition, but they continued to pound the full length of the rebel position. It was having a dual effect of suppressing the Khampas on the heights and providing cover for their own soldiers who had crossed the river before the bridge's destruction.

Phuntsok was joined by Lobsang. The Khampa chief had been coordinating fire for the machine guns, and now looked to the Tibetan Army officer for orders.

"Keep moving your MG's around to avoid their artillery," urged Phuntsok, "I'm going to check on the mortars."

He ran two hundred yards to where the mortar crews were dispersed among a wide area of flat ground strewn with boulders. As he got there, he came across a small stream flowing with crystal clear water from the melting snow above. He suddenly became aware that he had a raging thirst from his exertions during the battle, and from breathing the dry, thin air.

He sank down to his knees and drank his fill, then removed his cap and splashed water over his head. As he wiped away the cold and invigorating fluid from his face, he looked upward, following the course of the stream all the way up to the pockets of melting ice dotted over the pale brown slope a thousand feet above.

Images from the horror and devastation behind him filled his mind, and he felt a surge of shame wash over him. To Phuntsok, the mountain peak far above became a symbol of inaccessible aspiration – of achieving the highest ideals that human beings can achieve. His sense of failure to attain those goals brought on a deep-seated shame. The millennia of peaceful and compassionate lives that had been lived by his ancestors were calling him to account. The haunting voices reached deep down, beseeching the child inside him to stop the violent calamity that was encroaching on the sanctuary of the mountain.

He began to cry.

In an earlier, more peaceful time, he may not have been able to stop the sobbing brought on by such guilt and shame, but now, the madness of the battle beckoned him back to the stone hard reality of the war.

He got up and continued toward the sound of mortar fire, finding that the moment of retrospection had cleared his mind, but it had not cleansed his soul.

The ground on which the M-30 4.2-inch mortars were deployed was an area of level, smoothly eroded granite. As he hurried over, Phuntsok tried to disguise his reddened eyes from Ji-zhu who was in command of the mortar crews. The Teacher noticed Phuntsok's distress and barked an order to his squads to continue firing at will.

He took the Lieutenant by the shoulders and asked, "Phuntsok! Are you alright?"

Phuntsok nodded, still trying to shake off his emotions, but the concern on Ji-zhu's face had a disarming effect and he found he still couldn't speak.

Ji-zhu took a firmer hold, trying to shore up the Tibetan's vigour, "What's happened? Did your gunners take many casualties?"

Phuntsok looked up at the man revered by the Khampas as the closest link they had to the Dalai Llama and the way of life his people cherished before the Chinese invasion.

"Casualties?" he murmured, "... yes ... but not many. We disengaged and have relocated to save the guns."

"Then your distress I sense is from something less tangible?"

The sounds of battle resonated around them, but under Ji-zhu's gaze it seemed to Phuntsok as though he were momentarily buffered from the mayhem.

Phuntsok bowed his head, "I am ashamed Ji-zhu. Ashamed of my part in all of this ... this *insanity* ... ashamed of failing to find some way to avoid the killing as we Buddhists know we should. I feel that we have let the Dalai Llama down and disappointed his hopes for a peaceful solution to this war."

Phuntsok couldn't hear Ji-zhu's patient sigh above the sounds of battle all around them, but he heard his words as clearly as if they were alone on the mountainside.

"You are right to be disappointed my friend ... but the shame should belong to the Chinese. They are the aggressors here – not us."

A nearby explosion caused them both to reflexively hunch over, and Ji-zhu put an arm around the lieutenant as he led him toward the cover of a large boulder. They bobbed down as more enemy rounds landed in their vicinity, searching out the rebel mortars which were taking a toll on the communist troops on both sides of the river.

"Remember ..." said Ji-zhu raising his voice, "... we can only save our culture, and all that the Dalai Llama stands for – if someone defends it from this evil! If there is no-one else who can do this – and no other way to protect and preserve our innocence ... then we must do it ourselves!"

Phuntsok raised his head, his doubt and internal turmoil were soothed, but not completely. He nodded, "I understand. Thank you, Ji-zhu – I should not question that what we are doing is right ... but still, it all feels so wrong."

"It is the same for us all. The best we can do is try to find some peace within ourselves once we are forced into this madness."

The cough of mortars firing resounded across the rocky landscape, but it was answered minutes later by another salvo from the enemy artillery. As the shells screamed down, the two Tibetans flattened themselves against the hard ground. Fragments of hot metal bit into the rock above them and Phuntsok let out a gasp, his body going limp.

Ji-zhu sat up and pulled the lieutenant closer, checking for wounds. Blood began to soak through Phuntsok's tunic around a hole in his back at heart level. As more explosions erupted, one of the mortar crews disappeared inside one of the blasts. Smoke and dust subsided to reveal a scorched and empty granite surface, devoid of any life, or signs that a weapon had been firing from there.

Ji-zhu took a med-kit out of a pocket on Phuntsok's fatigues, and hurriedly applied a dressing to stop the bleeding. The shell fragment had struck him in the back, passing right through and shattering his collar bone as it exited the front of his chest.

The lieutenant came to, reaching for the stabbing pain in his chest with an agonized expression on his face.

"It's alright" said Ji-zhu. "You are lucky it wasn't any lower or you would not have regained consciousness."

Phuntsok relaxed once Ji-zhu had given him an ampule of morphine. Shortly after, the shelling subsided to the sound of a gentle rain of dust and powdered grit.

Phuntsok got up and took Ji-zhu's arm, and the two went to check on the mortar crews. The bombardment had taken out another of the positions, leaving only a dented baseplate lying metres away from its broken and bent tube.

Among the surviving crews were a half-dozen wounded, and Ji-zhu ordered them all to withdraw from the plateau to prevent them from taking any further casualties. As his men hurriedly loaded their pack horses with the dismantled mortars, Ji-zhu helped Phuntsok away from the area. He sought out Lobsang who assigned an infantryman to wrap the wounded officer's arm.

The Khampa chief then kneeled at the plateau's edge and watched as the last of the Chinese on the near side of the river were mopped up. He looked back up at the pair, his eyes reflecting sadness from their losses, but his expression was also tinged with some relief that the fight was now almost over, "It is finished soon," he said in a no-nonsense tone. "Our mortars and machine guns have done much damage to enemy below."

He pointed to the north-west, back in the direction from which they'd travelled along the trail from their main camp. Down below, a column of Khampas were moving toward them through the narrow strip of forest that fringed the river.

"Company of men sent along riverbank will soon finish Chinese."

"Good" said Ji-zhu, "... but the communists will not stop what they have been attempting here."

He indicated in the opposite direction, to the south-east where the river valley continued out of sight between steep slopes of bare, grey-brown rock, "They will simply try again a few miles downstream ... trying to keep us pinned here so that their main army can keep advancing toward Lhasa."

Lobsang got up and spat in the direction the Chinese positions.

"So be it! We hold them here and hope we slow main Chinese army!"

Ji-zhu turned to Phuntsok, "You must go back to headquarters with the rest of the wounded. We will radio Colonel Blackett and advise our situation. I expect he will want us to prevent any further attempts to cross the river as long as it does not stretch our forces too far apart."

Phuntsok gave a pained and shoddy salute with his good arm, and then joined the rest of wounded who were being readied for the hike back to camp. Ji-zhu and Lobsang went to a dug-in command post to radio a report to Blackett.

"We start moving men away from ledge so they will have cover from shelling" said Lobsang.

"Yes, but it will only be temporary...until we need to follow the Chinese to the site of their next crossing attempt" replied Ji-zhu. He looked a little further up the mountain, to the trail from which the goat track had split off from to reach the plateau, continued on around the slope. *More trekking … more fighting. The Khampas will need all their resolve to keep up this fight,* he thought sombrely.

As he glanced up at the snow-covered peak above, he too could feel the grief that Phuntsok had been feeling. But he stifled it with his own determined resolve to keep on going – it was a lack of compassion that he knew the current Dalai Llama – the reincarnation of the Bodhisattva of Compassion, would sanction. *His teachings would agree with the Khampa resistance,* he thought. *Why waste compassion on those who are unrepentant and do not deserve it?*

In his travels he had seen the results of allowing the evils of communism to decimate other cultures such as the Uighur, which the CCP was consuming as it spread its ideology into East Turkistan.

Man's inhumanity toward man at its worst.

Although he considered himself a peaceful man, he had no qualms about defending the way of life, and the homes and families of those among which he'd spent his childhood. To the death if necessary.

CHAPTER TWENTY-TWO

Supreme Command Union of Nations Forces – Asia (UNAS-COM) HQ
Dai Ichi Building
Tokyo,
Japan
June 8th, 1949

General Douglas MacArthur was uneasy but refused to let any of the officers assembled in the conference room see it. He strode confidently to the front of the room and began his presentation by pointing to the large wall map of the Russian Far East.

As his wooden pointer rested on the coastline west of Vladivostok, he glanced searchingly at those seated in the front row. These men, some of the highest-ranking officers in the US armed forces, needed to be convinced that his plan for the assault on Soviet-held territory, would be a successful one.

"Gentlemen, we have been tasked by the Union of Nations to assist with the ongoing conflict between the forces of the Republic of Russia and those of the renegade Soviet army, here in the Russian Far East."

The pointer moved onto the port city of Vladivostok, "The Soviets have fortified their defensive stronghold here, but the bulk of their land forces are now concentrated further to the north around Dalnerechensk, as they continue to push the Russians back toward Khabarovsk."

He paused, noting the expression on the face of the Chairman of the Joint Chiefs of Staff, General Omar Bradly. It was he who would be the most difficult to persuade, and by making it perfectly clear that the situation on the mainland was tenuous at best, MacArthur could then focus the attention of the JCS on what he perceived to be the vulnerability of the Soviets on the coast. He knew he was competing against the plan favoured by Washington, which was to join the Russians at Khabarovsk by sending troops and armour across land from Europe, but that would take months to assemble. He and his staff, most of whom had been in far-eastern Asia for years, knew they didn't have that much time if they wanted to seize the most important prize in the region – the port facilities at Vladivostok.

"The Soviets have taken their aggressive stance in the north, to ensure the security of their main line of supply; the railway line from China ... which crosses the border here at Suifenho ... and links up to the Trans-Siberian railway ... here at Ussuryisk, sixty miles north of Vladivostok."

He tapped around quickly from place to place, conscious that the JCS were well aware of the motivations behind the Soviet dispositions, and not wanting to waste their time on what they already knew.

"The Soviets have been successful in holding this region from the Russians, in part because of the vast distances the Russian Army has had to traverse for its supply. However, my planning staff and I believe that their success so far will now lead to their downfall."

MacArthur checked Bradley again, the JCS Chairman's attitude was unreadable behind the lenses of his glasses. The two representatives from the Navy, Admiral Louis A. Denfield – the Chief of Naval Operations, and Admiral Arthur W. Ranfield, the Vice CNO, had both been displaying a positive interest so far. The next stage of the presentation would see where they really stood.

The pointer went back down to Vladivostok, "The Soviets have mined the wharves inside the port, and there are a number of fortifications with heavy coastal guns located around the approaches. Over here ... directly across the gulf to the east from Vladivostok, there are several other defensive positions, including a small port here at Bol'shoy Kamen."

He turned to his audience, "These defences would all provide opposition to any landings in the area, along with a further small offshore force on Sakhalin Island comprised of naval troops and a few patrol boats."

He nodded to the two Admirals, "As you would be aware, the Soviets did not persuade any significant Russian naval forces to join their cause."

He returned to the map, "So ... we can see that the Soviets have focussed their efforts to the north, and around the land approaches to the perimeter of the city of Vladivostok. They understand that Vlasov's Russian Navy poses little threat to them as it is still in a rebuilding phase after its destruction during the wars in Europe. Consequently, the Soviets have left the coastline of Peter the Great Gulf lightly defended ... there are just too many miles for them to fortify effectively, and their strategy would not have required them to consider an attack from the sea by the Russians, who are still not capable of mounting amphibious operations."

The Admirals both acknowledged MacArthur's summary affirmatively. Bradley just gazed at the map, deep in his own reflections.

MacArthur straightened to his full height, gathering himself to deliver the most compelling line of his argument,

"Of course, the Soviets were not to know that the Union of Nations would be sending *us* to intervene."

He pivoted around and struck the map with a loud whack, "If we strike here!...at these two points ...", he exclaimed loudly as his cane smacked on two wide expanses of beach across the gulf from Vladivostok, "at Nakhodka Bay on Trudny Peninsula ... and at Livadiya to the west of Trudny ... with an invasion fleet launched from Japan – the Soviets will be exposed and find themselves fighting a war on two fronts. We have code-named this grand amphibious assault, 'Operation Freehand'."

Admiral Denfield asked the obvious question, "We've read your staff's report, but can you confirm that those landing sites have been thoroughly evaluated?"

"Yes", MacArthur answered patiently, "Admiral Barbey's staff have produced a comprehensive plan, including depth soundings taken by submarine, expected tides on the proposed landing dates, reconnaissance of enemy defences and complete detail of the Seventh Amphibious Fleet's logistical requirements for the transport during the first phase of the operation of two Marine divisions and the 1st Cavalry Division. The build-up for this operation will be cloaked by the current activity in Japanese ports to supply the ongoing UoN intervention in Korea."

Denfield and Radford both looked across to Admiral Daniel Barbey sitting at the end of the row. Barbey had attained fame within the Navy for his innovative and highly efficient leadership of MacArthur's sweeping advance across the western Pacific against the Japanese. He had also facilitated the return of many thousands of demobilised Japanese soldiers to Japan from China after the Pacific War had ended. All those operations had given him invaluable experience in the region.

MacArthur added, "Daniel will be providing you all with a more detailed briefing immediately following my own."

General Bradley stirred, announcing his intention to interrupt, and MacArthur paused to allow him to speak. "Douglas, what you've shown with regard to the Soviets all seems very plausible", he conceded. "I tend to agree that their land forces will be overextended if we land where you're suggesting ... but what about the Chinese?"

MacArthur had been expecting this response from Bradley. The threat from the Chinese being in relatively close proximity to the landing beaches, would be the major reason for committing the UoN land forces by land via railway through Siberia instead of by sea.

Bradley continued, "The Union of Nations Security Council has expressed concerns that Chinese support for the North Koreans may escalate to the use of ground troops there. Up in Russia, I'm more concerned they may provide air support to the Soviets – and we do not have a mandate to bomb the Chinese airfields in Manchuria, or for that matter, bomb their probable route across the Yalu River into North Korea – if either of those scenarios pan out."

"General Bradley, I appreciate your concerns" said MacArthur respectfully, then he rolled the dice.

"My response to those points is that we have prepared a secondary operation in our planning – a pre-emptive assault to ensure the capture of the port facilities at Vladivostok – *intact.*"

He let the significance of his proposal sink in. The primary report prepared for the JCS by his staff had detailed how the Soviets had prepared to disable the wharves by placing freighters at specific point along each of the docks. Each of the ships was mined with explosive charges which would sink them in place and render the facilities useless for weeks or possibly months.

"This secondary operation, to be conducted by British commandos and the US 10th Special Forces Group, will prevent the sabotage of the docks. It will thus ensure that after the landings we will immediately have at our disposal, a fully operational, major port facility from which we can escalate our campaign against the Soviets, and if necessary, against China."

Bradley's eyes widened behind his spectacles, giving him the appearance of a startled owl, "Well, I can't wait to see more on *that* little operation Douglas ... when you will be sharing that with us?"

"We didn't want to include it in the initial report you received without having determined that there was in fact a major landing to support. I must stress, that it is critical to the entire operation that Washington approves our planning, and that we move this along with all rapidity. We must strike with all speed now! So that we can obtain the benefits from the element of surprise before the Soviets have any inkling of what we're about to do."

He nodded to an aide who distributed copies of the secondary Vladivostok operation to the JCS.

"This plan has been fully prepped and ratified by the commanders of all units detailed to take part ... and has been sanctioned by the newly formed 'agency' – the CIG, who are responsible for developing unconventional warfare units in the United States."

Bradley was more of a dedicated 'conventional' warfare supporter, and scowled at the mention of the CIG. "Yes, yes ... I've heard of these units and all of their new methods ... but we will need to give final approval before this little side operation goes ahead."

"Of course, General ... Admiral Barbey will be including it in his more detailed briefing."

MacArthur was satisfied that he was still in control of the proceedings, and then went about the next phase of his presentation. He looked to the two Naval Operations Admirals, as though seeking their assistance with his next proposition.

"It is difficult for us to be too specific at a stage where there may only be contingency plans required for the probable aggression by the Chinese, so we should only allow for that possibility in our long-term strategy. As far as the landings are concerned, I believe Admiral Radford can shed some light on the newly increased capacity of our naval support."

The Admiral was a little surprised by the suggestion, but knew exactly what the wily General MacArthur was implying.

Radford turned to Bradley with a shrewd look on his hawkish features.

"I expect the General is referring to our new super-carrier – the USS United States ... which will now be available to support these landings," he said with a hint of pride. "It has just completed its sea trials and has taken on board three squadrons of Marine F9F-2 Panther jet fighters, and a squadron of F2H-2 Banshee fighter bombers."

Bradley got the message. The new super-carrier was by far the most potent projection of naval air power ever built. With a flight deck that hosted four catapults, and the traditional 'island' superstructure built flush with the deck, it could launch and retrieve twice as many aircraft as any previous class of carrier. Bradley knew of the political struggle to get the budget approved for the new carrier, made more difficult by strong objections from Army, due to what it perceived to be the advent of an age of nuclear warfare, where there would be no place for conventional weapons platforms such as large carriers. However, the Navy had finally won out, ironically aided by the influence of one of the Army's most notable sons – General Douglas MacArthur.

Bradley eyed MacArthur cautiously, "It looks like you had more than just a hunch we would need the extra firepower that the USS United States would give us for this kind of operation?"

MacArthur gave a slight smirk, not wanting to appear too smug at the success of his contribution to the budgeting process. As he was about to explain, his reasoning had been perfectly sound, "Well General, I'm sure you appreciate how it works ... while 3rd Army was under your wing and you kept watch over George Patton all those years in Europe – you can't always guess what your commanders are thinking."

Bradley chuckled laconically. Patton was a completely different temperament to his own. He'd learnt from experience that the only way to bring out the best in such a soldier was to just let out the reins and give him his head. The JCS Chairman got up and walked up to the map, hands on his hips, staring thoughtfully up at the jagged relief of the coastline MacArthur was proposing to assault.

"Well Douglas ... just what was it you said to those politicians that tipped the balance in favour of building that super-carrier?"

"I told them that for nations to live securely under the umbrella of nuclear deterrence – they will have to be prepared to fight a conventional war."

Bradley stood in respectful awe of this man of destiny. One who had been intended for military leadership from birth and had been instrumental in the defeat of the Japanese in the Pacific. The JCS chief was thinking of the current attitude of the Union of Nations toward the use of nuclear weapons, and their efforts to prevent their proliferation which had resulted in an edict to restrict their use in any conflicts sanctioned by the Security Council.

"A future where only conventional wars are fought, although the combatants have weapons of mass destruction at their disposal?" said Bradley. "It's a bit of a paradox wouldn't you say?"

"Yes, but it makes sense that nations would fear using such a destructive weapon. Wars will be fought as they have been since the Great War – with the intent of destroying the enemy's war production, and hence his capability to continue the fight – but only if your own civilisation is not destroyed in retaliation."

Bradley pursed his lips, finished musing over the map, and then returned to his seat. "Alright Douglas, I'm fairly certain our colleagues here from the Navy are on-board for this operation ... so you can count on my support when we try to convince the others in the JCS and the administration in Washington that your plan is a sound one."

"Thank you General."

"In the meantime, you can start moving the two Marine divisions and 1st Cavalry to Japan. Then get onto the 3rd Army Chief of Staff, Maj. General William Chase, to get his opinion as to which of his divisions are at the highest level of readiness, and that he recommends for the follow-up waves in the landings."

Once Bradley was on board, MacArthur knew how pivotal his influence could be in keeping things rolling. He was feeling more and more relieved, and confident that Freehand would be a success as the JCS Chief continued.

"I will point out however, that the major hurdle we'll have to overcome with convincing Washington is their fear of provoking a wider conflict with the Chinese," explained Bradley.

"That's why you're in that seat Omar," said MacArthur, "...and not someone like myself or General Patton ... we seem to bring out much more defensive reactions from those in public office. After all, politicians are wholly dependent upon their popularity for their positions – and taking risks of this magnitude can invoke great fear in their public."

Bradley just smiled coyly. MacArthur had been expecting a tougher struggle to get his superior to change his mind from supporting the Army's recommendation for bolstering the Russians by crossing Siberia. He wondered if Bradley had any inkling of just how strong a position the landings were going to put the UoN forces in, should the Chinese commit their ground forces to the war.

With a renewed vigour, and the surety that his own optimism would propagate to the others involved in Operation Freehand, he handed over to Admiral Barbey for the detailed briefing on the amphibious and special forces operations.

CHAPTER TWENTY-THREE

*"We have learned that the only policy suited to free
and enlightened men is to be sovereign over one's
own affairs and not to have the ridiculous
pretension of imposing it on others."*
Charles-Maurice de Talleyrand-Périgord

Mojave City,
2268 CE

A blanket of serenity wrapped itself around Eya as she
watched Arjon trim a few branches from a juvenile Cape
Myrtle with a laser scalpel. She loved it when he took time
away from his work to help in the garden.

Hesta announced that Thiessen had arrived and that
she'd asked him to wait in the atrium. Eya waited for Arjon
to respond but he was enjoying himself so much he didn't
want to leave. Finally, she prompted him, "You should go
and meet him before he has to ask Hesta where we are."

"Ah yes" he said absent-mindedly, then he kissed her
lightly on the cheek. "We'll be back in time for dinner to-
night."

"Good ... I'll pick something fresh to go in the rata-
touille!"

Arjon felt a twinge of regret at leaving. Their time together in the garden was precious to him, and as he walked
toward the atrium, he felt what could only be described as
separation anxiety. He realised that he appreciated being
with Eya more intensely now because of the stress that his

work for the Directory had been causing him, particularly due to using the Immerser to experience the Tibetan genocide.

He left the vibrant harmony and open expanses of the sunlit garden and entered the more secluded surrounds of the atrium's ivy-covered columns. The tinted, transparent roof let in a filtered and bronzed light that welcomed visitors, and a small fountain with some tropical fish meandering beneath the lilypads at its centre gave them something to enjoy while they waited.

"Arjon!" Thiessen sang out joyfully, "So good to see you after so long!"

Memories of the Enlightenment of the Free World War came flooding back to Arjon, and he was filled with a sense of excitement at the thought of working with his friend from the Centre of Truth once more.

"How're going Thiessen! It's been too long! Come into the den – I've a lot to share with you" Arjon replied enthusiastically.

They went to the den and chatted over some refreshments.

"Coralex has invited us to visit her at the headquarters of the Directory of Purpose … she's sent one of their gravgliders to pick us up," said Arjon. "In the meantime, I'd like to share what I discovered about Tibet and the missing fragments of the past pertaining to Ji-zhu Geist."

As they finished watching a holographic rendering of the meeting with Ji-zhu at the monastery, Thiessen sat in thoughtful silence while he drank his tea.

"This is not what I'd been expecting after you called to invite me here and you mentioned you had 'met' with Ji-zhu."

He put his cup down and sunk back into the cushioned leather armchair. "Your call piqued my interest, so I did some research. What I found in the Centre's archives doesn't concur with what we've just seen."

"Oh? In what way?" asked Arjon.

"There are glaring discrepancies between Ji-zhu's character and his actions shown in this simulation, and those depicted by our recorded history."

The CoT field agent sat immobile, his hands clasped together in his lap, giving an impression of sage immutability. "According to those records, the Ji-zhu of our past – the one who contributed so much to the founding of our Pillars – was a pacifist who preached non-violence and love for your enemy," he said with grave concern. "That obviously contradicts any notion that he may have taken an active part in the Tibetan resistance as portrayed in the Directory's simulation."

Arjon was taken aback, "Well ... I know the image of Ji-zhu accepted by our society is that of a man of peace ... but I just assumed he adopted his conciliatory stance after the war with the Chinese communists."

"I don't see how the simulation could deduce that he fought as a rebel unless it had access to data that I did not find," Thiessen pointed out abruptly. "Psychological profiling theory shows that strong convictions toward non-violence are usually formed early in personality development. The fact that the simulation shows he demonstrated a willingness to fight for his people, regardless of his Buddhist upbringing, suggests he would not have had any pacificist tendencies in his psychological make-up. That is in direct contrast to our own history's description of him which relies on him always having been a pacifist!"

Arjon put his cup down on the coffee table and stayed leaning forward out of his chair, his face a picture of intrigue. "But when Hesta created the simulation for the Directory, wouldn't she have accessed the same public-facing archives from the Centre of Truth when formulating Ji-zhu's personality?"

"Yes ... and that's what's so disturbing," said Thiessen flatly. "For Hesta to have formulated a Ji-zhu who was not a pacifist, she must have accumulated some of the underlying data from a source within the CoT's archives that I have overlooked."

Growing more animated and gesturing with outstretched palms, the field agent continued with his observations, "It says to me that there is information contained within the meganet's neural network that was subsequently mined by Hesta – but was missed by my own investigation ... and she may have found a significant flaw in the accepted history of our society's founding!"

"Qwerty!" Arjon exclaimed. "But couldn't we determine where that data came from?"

Thiessen sighed at the magnitude of possibilities, "The source we are talking about is all of the data in the world! We may just as well say that the overall consensus of all of that accumulated data has led to the conclusion that Ji-zhu was a rebel!"

Arjon stood up and started pacing around, his brow creased with confusion. He could see cracks appearing in the altruistic rocks upon which his society's ethical, moral and philosophical foundations had been created, "This is terrible! I'm just an everyday citizen ... I'm not sure if I can handle the implications ... what are we going to do?"

Thiessen rose, at first into a slumping posture as he too felt the burden of their findings. Then he straightened,

THE FREE WORLD WAR II – A Probability of Evil

standing like a sentinel guarding the gates to the sanctum of Truth he represented. "Do not concern yourself with this any further. Please continue with your research and report to me often."

"Of course ... but what about the data in your archives?"

"That will be my concern." Thiessen's disposition changed from guardian to that of an intrepid sleuth. "As you will recall, the Enlightenment of the Free World War pointed to a discrepancy between the revelations around General Patton and our accepted history. Ever since then, I have had suspicions that there may have been other tampering with our history ... and this is the first time an opportunity to pursue its sources has presented itself."

Arjon shook his head in disbelief. The Centre of Truth was the Pillar upon which all the others depended. Truth was core to the principles that united humanity. Trust in the CoT was the key component that bound the other Pillars together, and hence all of the utopian civilisation's people lived with the harmonious certainty that their opinions and actions were guided by the same trusted sources, leaving little room for division or conflict.

Arjon the enlightened citizen was not feeling very empowered. He stopped pacing and felt a tremor in his bones. *This implies that at some time in the dark past before our founding, or even after that ... someone or something may have tainted the data used by the Centre of Truth.*

The possibility made him feel something he rarely felt – anger.

A chime sounded and Hesta advised that the DoP glider had arrived for them.

"Oh ... well, our flight awaits" said Arjon with some discomfort considering the gravity of the conversation he and Thiessen had been having.

"Fine" said Thiessen curtly, although his mind was clearly on other matters. As they walked out to the front of the bower, he put a finger to one side of his nose and warned Arjon, "We must be extremely careful about what we have just discussed ... be very discreet while talking on the Directory's glider in case anything is being recorded."

Minutes later the two were airborne and speeding at great velocity over the American mid-west toward the DoP facility in the Rocky Mountains. The ten-seater executive grav-glider used an ultra-mass anti-gravity drive, and inside the cabin the two passengers could clearly hear the rush of air outside as there was no sound coming from the craft's propulsion.

"We should be there in half an hour," said Arjon checking his hand-held.

He glanced through the wide viewport and down onto the vast expanse of green grassland below. "I never tire of seeing the Great North American Prairie from the air," he said with admiration. "To think that all these millions of square miles used to be covered in wheat crops stretching almost all the way up to the arctic ... such a waste."

"Agreed. Restoring it to its natural state was a major step forward in saving this region's wildlife – and its environment," replied Thiessen.

The scenery far below gave Arjon cause for reflection. "When I was a boy, I wanted to be a cowboy out here ... riding a horse and going hunting out on the range for days at a time. It would have been just like it was many hundreds of years ago ... except of course for the refrigerated wagons to store the meat."

"Boyhood dreams ... they seem so innocent went we look back on them. Could you really have made a living that way?" asked Thiessen.

"Sure. You still can now, but the preferred mode of transportation is motorised for the bigger companies. The herds of cattle and bison number in the tens of millions ... all perfectly healthy and running around as nature intended. You just need a hunting permit, or else work for a supplier."

"It makes sense, free-range meat tastes so much better than the alternative," said Thiessen.

"Mmmm ... but no doubt most of the harvesting is now done by robots. Still, the opportunity is there if that is the way you want to earn a livelihood."

A chime sounded and the glider's AI advised that a call was coming through from Coralex. She appeared on a viewscreen, sitting at her desk with her hair in a neat chignon. Behind her on the wall of her office was the banner of the Directory of Purpose. It was an ancient-looking tapestry of a tree showing four outward reaching branches depicting the first four Pillars, with the main trunk of the Directory now connecting and sustaining them.

The Directory's banner suggested established tradition, in contrast to its newly sprouted existence. As she smiled brightly, Coralex saw the serious expressions on the faces of the two men seated in the glider, and asked, "Is this a good time for a call? I thought if we could make some headway now it would leave more time for you to tour our new facility."

"Yes ... yes certainly" said Arjon. "This is Thiessen, a field agent from the Centre of Truth."

The three continued with an introduction to each of their backgrounds, which led to the subject of their current work.

"Coralex will be involved with my project to confirm what we know of the events surrounding the formation of the Pillars," Arjon explained to Thiessen.

The CoT agent was curious, "And what does the Directory hope to learn from this research?"

"We expect this project will provide us with a more detailed historical background, and deeper insights to assist us to further develop our role as the Pillar who will be guiding and coordinating the others," replied Coralex.

Thiessen glowered at the thought of oversight by another Pillar on the sacrosanct source of integrity of his CoT. Although he had played a part in the events that led to the Directory's inception, by way of his contribution to the Enlightenment of the Free World War, he was wary of any entity that could potentially create an imbalance with the previous equilibrium. The Spire of Evolution, Union of Nations and the Bureau of Sanity had always looked to the Centre of Truth for verification of their edicts.

Thiessen's voice did not betray any concern as he sought clarification from the first representative he had ever talked to from the Directory. "Could you please elaborate on your particular role, and how you expect to contribute to your Pillar's goals?"

"I'd be delighted," said Coralex in a professional manner. "As Arjon may have already told you, my research will at first be focussed on the missing elements of the founding of our Pillars. I have qualifications in anthropology, psychology, philosophy and also theology. Much of that content has been uploaded using the accelerated learning functionality provided by the latest Immersers."

Her statements advised the other two that she possessed the knowledge in each of her fields of study, equivalent to what could previously have only resulted from a whole lifetime of learning.

"Interesting" said Thiessen, "I have not personally indulged in increasing my cognitive abilities by using the

Immerser. Why do you think it has been more effective than the previous methods of memory upload?"

"Ah, that lies in the enhanced synaptic connection of the Immersers," she replied. "There is an old proverb regarding how humans learn ... it goes, 'I hear ... I forget; I see ... I remember; I *do* ... I *understand*'. It explains that instead of listening to lectures, or watching demonstrations, we learn best by actually *experiencing* the methodology for each field of study that is uploaded – it replicates the crucial process of using that information to solve problems, and to pass examinations."

"That's most impressive" said Arjon. "I'll be taking it more seriously in future if I need to interview a research assistant who looks like a teenager, but they tell me they have twenty years experience."

Coralex smiled at Arjon's levity, and she also began to feel more at ease in the presence of Thiessen. It was rare for anyone to encounter an official from the mysterious and closeted Centre of Truth. She continued with her response to his question, "The Directory has assigned me to work with Arjon and the simulation produced by Hesta because of my expertise in those related fields. The origin of the Pillars, and the contribution made by Ji-zhu Geist, are the areas of particular interest to me, and considering my background, I will also be concentrating on what we can learn from Ji-zhu with regard to the Enlightenment of the Soul."

She took a sip from a glass of water and then clasped her hands together in front of her as though about to pray. "The Directory has stated as its primary goal, that of becoming a provider of guidance to the other Pillars. In doing so, we must consider all facets of human thought in our epistemology – both secular and spiritual. We will also be framing our own strategy to ensure that it aligns with that of the other Pillars."

She sounded confident, and her countenance suggested she was unfazed by the magnitude of the Directory's task. "We intend to be the navigator of their course, not the captain. That role will as always be performed by the people. We realise that a society of empowered and enlightened individuals is only possible with the absence of any overbearing power structures in our lives. The Pillars are not there to tell you what you can or cannot do – but simply to guide us on our journey."

Thiessen nodded encouragingly. One of the CoT's fundamental principles was that its members were servants of the Truth, nothing more.

Coralex took another sip. She hadn't been expecting to share the entirety of the brief but important story of the DoP but felt it necessary in order to include the others who would be working with her on her mission. "As you know, the civil administration function of every nation on earth is now run by the global network of AIs. Some may say this leaves room for the Directory of Purpose to fill the space that was once taken by each of those nation's governments. That leadership function to which humans previously looked, where an assembly such as a democratic party, monarchy or other power structure, once presided in authority above them. We have no intention of assuming such a position. That role is now taken by each and every one of us." She smiled with pride and added, "You are the leader of your own life."

"Wonderful!" Arjon said with glee. "I'm enthralled by the Directory's prospects for the future if it's comprised of people such as yourself!"

Thiessen was grudgingly impressed. "I too am encouraged. It seems that the function of this new Pillar will also be one which simply educates and advises."

The glider began to descend and Arjon gazed out of his viewport at the sea of green grassland as it suddenly washed up against the rising pinnacles of the Rocky Mountains. There was snow on many of the higher peaks, and the shadowed valleys were filled with the near-black forests of evergreens in mid-summer.

Coralex noted the glider's position from one of the screens in front of her, "Ah, I see you're almost here. I'll meet you at the landing pad."

The grav-glider continued its descent beyond the outer edge of the massive mountain range, and deep into the vast, remote interior filled with jagged peaks, rivers and forests. A short time later, a towering mountain loomed up ahead, distinct from the dozens surrounding it by its chiselled, almost smooth grey outline.

As they drew closer, Arjon gasped as he noticed the outer surface of the mountain's conical upper slopes were bedecked with man-made features such as balconies, ledges and wide viewing portals. Those features below the treeline were connected by winding walkways lined with firs and pines, and several much larger openings hosted landing pads. The mountain's summit was a cap of reflected brilliance, not from the pure white snow of some of the higher mountain peaks beyond it, but from a flurry of metallic silver antennae and large satellite dishes pointing skyward.

As the grav-glider slid gracefully into one of the openings and sank silently onto the pad, Coralex walked out and greeted her visitors.

They toured the facility, travelling by mag-lev cars along a series of tunnels which linked the mountain's myriad chambers. The reasoning behind selecting the interior of a mountain for their headquarters soon became apparent, as many of the chambers were filled with vast banks of quantum supercomputers, servers and communications equipment – the hardware requirements for generating the next era of simulations. Apart from the efficiencies gained from keeping all of the computers cooled deep underground, the mountain was situated above a source of geothermal power, supplied by the same magma-heated artesian water which fed the many hot springs in the region.

As they stopped for lunch on one of the balcony restaurants, they admired the epic view of the mountain range from twelve thousand feet.

"Whew!" exclaimed Arjon, "I thought I had it good looking out onto a forest from the window of my den … but this is amazing!"

"We are all of us very thankful to live and work out here with all this natural beauty," replied Coralex.

"Live?" asked Thiessen, "Inside the mountain?"

"Oh no, many of us live among the nearby mountains. It's very convenient even in winter when the entire range is buried under dozens of feet of snow."

"Ah yes, the advantages of having aircars," said Thiessen.

They sat at a sunlit corner table and ordered lunch. Behind them on the wall hung the same ancient-looking tapestry of a tree from Coralex's office, and below it, the Directory's mantra written in an archaic font: 'Who you were; Who you are; Who you will be'.

Thiessen was curious about a remark Coralex had made on the flight up, and so asked, "Why do you see the Enlightenment of the Soul as being important to your work?"

Arjon added quickly, "Yes ... I noticed you brought up the subject of reincarnation with Ji-zhu at the monastery ..."

Coralex recalled warmly her encounter with the iconic figure from their past. "It's not by coincidence that we're following that line of investigation," she advised. "Billions of human beings – most of them endowed with a reasonable level of intelligence – believe in the existence of things which have not been proven by science. We have proven that we have a soul ... but what are the implications of that? Before the Enlightenment of the Soul, the vast majority of people already believed in the existence of some form of spiritual procession or after-life."

Personally, Thiessen had an open mind on the subject, but his position with the CoT forced him to categorise such concepts so that they did not conflict with his work. "I agree that the metaphysical is an area of conjunction, but also of contention between science and spiritualty" he said flatly. "I'll be following your research that uses these new, more powerful simulations with a great deal of interest."

Coralex nodded. Receiving any recognition, even conditionally, from a representative of the Centre of Truth was progress in the right direction. The CoT was the entity her Directory saw as the most challenging to work with. "We see the role of artificial intelligence and the simulations it is generating, as integral to our research," she explained. "As you both would know, when a computer plays chess it accesses historical data such as the opponent's previous games, and then uses it to calculate the probability that the move it makes next will be the best move to help it win. It is the same principal Hesta uses when she determines what you would like for dinner, based on the historical data she has about your preferences."

She leaned forward across the table, "The probabilities generated by machine-learning algorithms are the keys that are going to open an infinite number of doors."

She shifted her weight to one side and waved her hand at the DoP's mantra on the wall behind them.

"When determining the '*Who you will be*' – which applies not just to the individual, but also to humanity as a whole; it is those engines of probability that will provide us with the options that we will recommend to the other four Pillars. That in turn will be used to guide and hopefully improve our evolution; our sanity or reasoning; our union or social harmony; and of course – our integrity by way of the verifiable truth."

"Magnificent! Spectacular!" said Arjon barely able to contain his enthusiasm. To think that by way of his involvement with developing Hesta's first simulation, he had played a small but significant part in the Directory's founding. It was a source of unbridled joy for him, and now that he was to continue to contribute was even more uplifting.

Thiessen's thoughts were leading him along a slightly different line. Remembering the conversation he'd had with Arjon that morning about the discrepancies between the simulation of the Tibetan invasion and his own investigations into Ji-zhu's past, he could foresee where there may be flaws in this new Pillar's sources.

You are only as credible as the information you receive, he thought.

Arjon noticed how distracted his friend was and decided it was a good time for them to return to Mojave City.

"Coralex, thank you for your valuable time, but we have another engagement and must soon depart."

The tour ended, and the two visitors returned to Arjon's bower. Arjon left Thiessen with an aperitif in the lounge, and then went to help Eya prepare dinner in the kitchen. She was busy washing the vegetables she'd picked from her garden, "It's nice to have something hand-made for change," she said happily. "So much of what we consume is given to us by technology."

Arjon could see her point, with AIs and roboserves which also cleaned house, there was a nostalgic joy in making your own meals. As he began helping her, he thought of Coralex's description of the plans by the Directory to use advanced technology to navigate the course that humanity should take in the future, and wondered if one day in the far-flung future, humans would get the same nostalgic satisfaction from just thinking for themselves.

CHAPTER TWENTY-FOUR

Operation Mercury
Vladivostok,
Far East Russia
June 30th, 1949
0215 HRS

Lieutenant Mark Benson rolled back the sleeve of his wetsuit and checked his watch in the pitch darkness. The faint green glow of the luminous dial told him they were five minutes from zero hour. He tapped Sgt. Moore on the shoulder and they resumed paddling their kayak in rhythmic unison. The breeze was only light, so their progress across the harbour had been steady since being dropped off by the submarine. Benson looked astern and counted the silhouettes of the other canoes of No. 11 Commando Battalion trailing behind his. Each crew was following the luminous patches on the backs of the balaclavas of the crew in front of them. In the blackness beneath the tiny sliver of moon, it had been decided that the usual practice of tethering each craft to the one in front would slow them down when speed was critical. An hour ago, three Allied submarines had slipped quietly through the strait between Russky Island and mainland Vladivostok, and then taken only minutes to drop off their commando passengers outside the miles-wide mouth of the enemy-held harbour.

The decision not to tether the kayaks had paid off, as the few distant searchlights and a Soviet patrol boat had successfully been avoided as each of the commando teams paddled hard toward their respective targets.

Every fifteen minutes, Benson checked his compass, and then pulled out an infra-red sniper scope to help confirm their position. It had been hoped the new IR technology issued to the leader of each team would provide them with a more accurate method of reaching their target than a compass alone, considering the difficulties with navigating with no lights on the shore as reference points on a slowly moving tide. Through the scope, Benson felt relieved as he made out the dim greenish shape of a freighter straight ahead, and then tapped Sgt. Moore's shoulder to begin paddling again.

Zero hour. The crews stood off several hundred yards from the completely blacked-out wharf while they waited for the next crucial stage of the operation to begin.

Tense seconds passed, then they heard the drone of aircraft engines from a combined sortie of US and Russian heavy bombers. The whistle of falling bombs, and then the resounding concussions from multiple explosions inside the city, signified the start of the commando's attack.

With the dim glow from the growing fires started by the air-raid behind it, the barely visible outline of the freighter assigned to Benson's team loomed ahead. As they paddled quickly toward the wharf, the lieutenant did a mental check that the silhouette matched the one from the recon photographs taken only days before.

Minutes later, his kayak bumped softly against the hull, followed by the five others of his team which lined up along the length of the ship. Under the cover of the continuous thump of bombs from the air-raid, grappling hooks were thrown upwards, catching on the railings that ran along the edge the deck. The ten commandos then climbed the ropes to the top, where as expected, no Soviet sentries were posted due to the dangers of standing guard on a floating bomb during an air-raid.

Benson and Moore rushed straight up to the bridge, along with two members of the US Navy Underwater Demolition Team assigned to each ship. It was their responsibility to disable the demolition charges once they were found. Three others stayed on deck to cover the gangway, while three went below to begin raising steam. Intelligence from pro-Republican spies in the port had advised that all of the freighters were still operational because the Soviets were so confident from their successes against the Russian Army to the north, that they were expecting to use the freighters at a later date to expand the number of supply convoys between Vladivostok and China.

The door to the bridge was unlocked, and the Americans quickly confirmed that the ship's controls were functioning before heading to the hold to find the charges.

Benson checked his watch again ... 0315 HRS.

A voice piped up from the engine room, "Boilers have been lit – another twenty minutes till we have a head of steam."

One of the UDT men came back up from the hold, "We found the charges and cut the connections to the shore" he explained. "We found the fuse lines first ... had to follow them down to the bottom of the hold where the explosives were placed below the water-line. They would have blown the bottom of the ship out left no chance of repairing or re-floating it."

Benson nodded, "Let me know once you have your own detonators in place ... you'll have time to run the fuse wires up here once we get under way."

The plan was to get the ships away from the docks and at least out into the deeper waters away from the harbour's main channels, where they could be safely sunk if needed. There was a slim chance they might get the ships further out, even try to escape beyond the port altogether, but that would put them under the sights of the guns situated around the harbour. All of the volunteers for this mission were expecting to exit the ship, recover their kayaks which would still be tied to the railings, and risk getting captured once their job was done.

0330 HRS

The clamour from the air-raid and the responding anti-aircraft gunfire continued as Benson watched a signal lamp flutter briefly from a wharf on the opposite side of the harbour. One of the other freighters was about to get under way. They would all need to know once the first ship started leaving because of the impending reaction from the Soviets.

With his own ship now ready to make way, Benson leaned out of the hatchway and ordered the men posted on deck to detach the gangway and cast off the mooring lines.

He moved the engine telegraph's handle into position and then called the corresponding command down the voice-pipe, "Ahead one third!"

Sgt. Moore started turning the wheel as the freighter lurched sluggishly forward, bumping against the rubber tires cushioning the dock, and then slowly pulled away.

Shouts of alarm came from the shore, and then several shots rang out. A firefight ensued as the commandoes on deck returned fire at a group of Soviet guards who'd seen the ship begin to move off. On the bridge, one of the UDT men climbed up from below, unreeling a fuse line and then began connecting it to the box with the plunger that would set off the charges.

Within minutes, the freighter was slipping out of sight into the darkness of the main channel.

0355 HRS

Five of the six freighters had made their way out into the channel leading away from the docks, and then shifted their course to prevent their blocking the main channel if sunk. One ship had not been able to get under way, and most of its commandos had been taken prisoner.

Out in the harbour, the darkness turned to bright light as a number of star-shells were fired into the air by the shore batteries.

The first of the rusty old cargo ships was now under the guns of the Novosiltsevskaya Battery, but there was no immediate response. With his crew ready to blow the charges if they came under fire, Benson was thinking the Soviets may be hesitating, probably debating whether they should first send out patrol boats to try boarding and recapturing them.

Another minute passed before he got his answer. A flash from the shoreline was immediately followed by a huge geyser only yards away from the leading ship.

"Prepare to abandon ship!" Benson shouted out of the hatchway down to the men on the deck, then repeated the order into the voice-pipe.

The first freighter began to swerve toward the shore, and through his glasses Benson could see its commandos unfastening their kayaks and then begin jumping into the water. Another salvo from the big gun resulted in a hit amidships, and the ship seemed to halt momentarily, before it resumed its momentum. Benson knew that the team's commander would have stayed on board to set off the charges, and moments later a blast from below the waterline confirmed it. The front of the ship was lifted out of the water, then splashed back downwards sending a large wave rolling towards the kayaks nearby. The small craft were lifted up by the wave, but none capsized. With some relief, Benson then saw the last commando jump ship, realising that he would be doing the same in a matter of minutes.

Before they came under the guns of the other batteries covering the entrance to the harbour, all of the remaining teams began to head for shallow water and abandoned ship. Benson set off his charges and then jumped into the cold waters of Vladivostok harbour, not caring about the risk of hyperthermia but only that their mission had been a success.

There was nowhere to hide for the raiders, and they were soon rounded up by patrol boats and taken prisoner.

The end of Operation Mercury in the early hours of June 30th, 1949 heralded the dawn of the forthcoming day – a day that was to become the beginning of the end for the communists in the Russian Far East.

CHAPTER TWENTY-FIVE

"The experience of the last twenty years has shown that in peacetime the communist movement is never strong enough for the Bolshevik Party to seize power. The dictatorship of such a party will only become possible as the result of a major war."
Josef Stalin
19 August 1939

Nakhodka Bay,
Russian Far East
June 30th, 1949
0430 HRS

Pyotr stood in the dark, daydreaming of the next time he would be getting drunk under the bright lights in the tavern. It seemed to him that he'd become some kind of nocturnal animal, sleeping in the daytime and standing guard all night.

He felt a nudge on his arm as Grigori passed him a boiled potato. Their rations had been getting increasingly scarce as the struggle against Vlasov's army wore on.

"There is no meat again today," Grigori told him.

"No matter," Pyotr replied disconsolately. "We can check the traps by the stream after we get relieved ... there may be a rat, or if we are lucky – a vole."

"Ugh ... or else another one of those tiger snakes eating our catch," added Grigori.

Pyotr stood up, putting a piece of the potato in his mouth and peering out of the slit at the front of their earth and timber bunker toward the sea. There was still half an hour till dawn, so he could barely make out the white breakers from the choppy water being swept up by the wind onto the beach one hundred yards away.

He put his face to the scope which was mounted on a tripod, and saw nothing but a cloak of dark grey drizzle drifting down and obscuring the eastern horizon.

"Oh boze moi, it is not going to be any good for fishing either," he said.

"We may find some crabs once the tide goes out later on," said Grigori hopefully. "At least it is a hell of lot better down here than up in the north. Those poor bastards will get water-logged if it keeps raining."

"It is a swamp up at Dalnerechensk even without the rain," Pyotr pointed out. "They will not notice the difference."

He checked the time, 0500 HRS.

Another hour until the guard changes, then a couple of hours for other duties and then with luck some time for scavenging the shoreline before getting some sleep. Then another night watch. The same routine, night after night. It will be a month before we get a weekend pass and see the cosy inside and bright lights of the tavern in Vladivostok again.

He heard Grigori cocking the machine gun beside him. His comrade was taking station in readiness for the impending dawn. Pyotr put his eyes back to the scope and swept the dim line of the horizon. He held his breath as he thought he saw a glimpse of a distant shape, but the sky seemed to blend into the sea, so it was difficult to be sure.

He paused, holding his breath to keep the scope steady again, and strained hard to view the windswept sea more clearly, even though the drizzle was beginning to lighten up. Unable to confirm anything, he adjusted the focus and shifted the scope to the foreground where the waves were breaking over the tops of a line of submerged obstacles. The six-foot crossed-steel structures stretched away in a staggered line in either direction along the beach and would be fully exposed once the tide went out. Then one exploded.

The two sentries froze with alarm as they saw a deluge of water cascading down in the aftermath of the blast, and bent and twisted girders splashed back into the sea. Then another explosion destroyed a second obstacle, then another … and then multiple geysers erupted all along the shoreline as the demolition charges laid hours before by the frogmen of the 3rd Engineer Special Brigade destroyed the first line of beach defences.

Pyotr and Grigori watched in disbelief, and then with horror as farther out to sea, bright flashes appeared. At first only a few, then a constant, bright blinking that spanned the entire width of the bay.

Pyotr closed his eyes. He knew that in mere moments the naval gunfire would be turning his world into a cataclysm, and that those flashes on the horizon may well be the last bright lights he would ever see.

CHAPTER TWENTY-SIX

Operation Freehand
Peter the Great Gulf
June 30th, 1949
D-Day – 0600 HRS

The heavy cruiser USS Salem was barely rolling in the weak swell as Admiral Daniel Barbey stepped outside from the warm confines of the bridge and took hold of the railings on the bridge-wing. He peered skywards and was reassured by the disappearing clouds, and by the absence of flak. His memories of the kamikaze attacks in Leyte Gulf had been haunting him in the previous days.

The continual booming from the dozens of battleships and cruisers assembled for the landings was louder outside the bridge, and the soundwaves that pounded his eardrums hammered home to him the awesome firepower at the disposal of his fleet.

He turned to see the battleship USS Wisconsin, half a mile astern, momentarily disappear from view as her sixteen-inch guns unleashed a salvo towards the shore. Bright orange flame spewed out from the cloud of enveloping smoke and cast a reflection onto a sea brimming like the fires of hell.

The sound of the shells roaring overhead, each one weighing over a ton, caused Barbey to shiver. They would be joining the thousands of tons of high explosive from the other ships pouring down on the Soviet defences above the beach eight miles away, and onto those further inland.

He turned to the west and raised his binoculars. The flash of gunfire from the 7th Fleet off Vladivostok would be inflicting similar devastation on the beleaguered port city. However, their fire would be carefully avoiding the port facilities which had been saved from sabotage during the night by Allied special forces.

Barbey had only been remotely involved in the planning for Operation Mercury, but had received word upon waking that it had achieved its objectives. He was unaware of the casualty rate, or the fate of the sixty men who took part in the raid, but he knew there was little chance any would have escaped from the harbour. *At least the survivors can expect to be liberated soon if the landings succeed,* he thought sombrely.

He glanced at his watch. 0515 HRS.

The first wave were due to hit the beaches in thirty minutes. He pointed his glasses to the north, but struggled to get a clear view of the beach through the congested multitude of landing ships. Majestic scenes such as this never failed to impress him. Hundreds of troop transports, LSTs, LCIs and other transports and support vessels were waiting to take their turn and move in and unload after the initial waves of landing craft and amphibious armoured vehicles, or LVTs, had begun to establish a beachhead.

It was an intricate military orchestration so complex that very few individuals could comprehend it. Months of planning every finite detail and synchronised movement – every single ship, landing craft and platoon of men knew exactly what they were supposed to do, and when they had to do it.

The end result would be the delivery of hundreds of thousands of men, thousands of tanks, armoured and transport vehicles, and millions of tons of supplies to the shores of Na-khodka Bay.

The first to go in would be the 1st and 3rd Marine Divisions and the 1st Cavalry Division at Trudny Peninsula. After establishing the beachhead, they were to strike inland and to the west, securing the landing zone's left flank at Abrek Bay. From there, the allies would push to the north before wheeling around to assault Vladivostok, the last stronghold of Russian communism.

The rising daylight brought with it a fresh breeze from the east. Barbey breathed in the air which was laden with a saltiness being whipped off the rising chop on the ocean. It gave his nostrils a momentary reprieve from the acrid smell of cordite and smoke and allowed some remembrance of humanity to return whilst still witnessing the scenes of ordered chaos and destruction all about him.

He went back inside where the Salem's captain, John C. Daniel, was quietly issuing orders to his bridge officers. As Capt. Daniel finished confirming a fire order for the forward turrets onto an enemy artillery battery five miles inland, Barbey caught his attention.

"Air reconnaissance giving the Salem enough inshore targets Captain?" asked Barbey.

"Sufficient for now Admiral," an officious Daniel replied, then added with a little more levity, "...but the fleet may need to send out a long-range Catalina to find us more once the Soviets have begun to retreat."

Barbey chuckled. He appreciated having such an accomplished officer in command of his flagship. He also relished having his pennant flying from such a modern and formidable warship as the Salem. The older cruisers that served the same purpose during his campaigns from New Guinea and then on toward Japan in the Pacific War had always seemed to be second-rate hand-me-downs from Nimitz's 7th Fleet.

0530 HRS

Barbey left the ship's bridge, heading through a hatchway and down to his own Admiral's bridge twenty feet below. This more spacious area performed a different function to the bridge above used by Capt. Daniel. It included the same kind of viewing area as the ship's bridge at its front, but the rearward space was adorned with charts, and there was a large table for displaying his fleet dispositions. It also hosted a large adjacent conference room where Barbey could brief all of the captains under his command at once.

A group of officers from his planning staff were hovering over the table and preparing to receive updates from the beaches once the first wave had landed. Barbey stopped to look through the sloped ports at the front of his bridge, as the next phase of Operation Freehand began.

A flotilla of specially converted LCIs following just behind the first wave of landing craft, started unleashing row after row of high-explosive rockets. The sky over the bay was suddenly filled with streaks of blue-white flame which arced upwards in waves and then descended onto the slightly elevated forest beyond the shoreline.

The admiral saw volley after volley being fired skywards, followed seconds later by the saturating blasts exploding among the most likely locations of the entrenched and bunkered communists in the trees above the sand-covered beaches. He watched with grim satisfaction as the enemy positions were engulfed by the highly concentrated and extremely destructive barrage.

Poor devils, he thought, and then turned to get an update from his staff before entering the conference room at the rear. Inside, General MacArthur was conferring over a map table with the commanders of the 1st, 3rd and 5th Marine Divisions, along with General Hobart Gay, the CO of the 1st Cavalry Division.

MacArthur looked up from his battlefield commanders conference as Barbey entered. He straightened his dignified frame and asked, "Everything still going according to schedule Admiral?"

"Like a very well-oiled machine General" replied Barbey. "The rocket LCIs are unloading right on time and the initial assault wave escorted by minesweepers and combat engineers are approaching the shore. The first ramps should be dropping in fifteen minutes."

Barbey saw the role of his 7th Amphibious Force in the overall landing operation as a massive exercise in timing. If one small part of the tightly scheduled sequence of events were to be held up, then a ripple effect would emanate all the way back through the following waves. His Admiral's bridge, and its connecting command and communication centres, were the nerve centre for the whole operation. His officers were being continually updated on the progress of the big ships such as the LSTs, and the scores of smaller craft out on the water. They in turn, would be keeping the Marines, 1st Cavalry and General MacArthur appraised of their respective units, and the overall progress.

It was a Navy operation, even on the beaches – right up until the land forces secured their perimeters.

The Admiral moved into the circle of officers gathered around the table, "Carrier-based air strikes are now hitting the Soviet artillery further inland."

He pointed to a region on the map, "Fleet air recon has detected new concentrations in the forests east of Fokino ... here – ten miles from the beaches."

Barbey looked up, conveying the concerns he had that the communists may be concealing more large calibre guns in the dense forest. "We think they may be holding their fire until the first wave reaches the beach."

A reserved MacArthur looked on, his hands on his hips, calculating the potential losses if Barbey's assumptions turned out to be correct. "Please give that possibility your utmost attention Admiral," he said calmly.

Barbey nodded and turned to his aide, ordering him to divert impending air strikes from his aircraft carriers onto the new targets.

MacArthur returned his attention to his Generals just as an adjutant handed him a signal which he duly read to the others. "The island of Putyatin lying offshore from Abrek Bay, has now been cleared of the enemy by the two companies of paratroopers from the 101st Airborne that dropped there during the early hours of this morning."

He moved to a wall map of the coastline, "On Sakhalin Island up here to the north-east, the battalion of US Rangers have encountered stiffer opposition than expected and have not yet reached the small harbour on the west coast. However, they advise that enemy resistance is weakening and should be mopped up within the next twenty-four hours. In addition, air recon confirms that the Soviet naval units stationed in the harbour have been destroyed by the earlier air attacks."

He studied the map as he called over his shoulder to Admiral Barbey, "I'm sure those few PT boats would not have got close enough to trouble your invasion fleet anyway Admiral."

His cane swept over the islands off the coast on the map, "With the outlying islands secure, we can be assured there'll be no interference to the main landings at Nakhodka and Livadiya."

It was a confirmation that an initial stage had been completed, rather than a significant milestone being reached, but MacArthur could now safely look ahead to the activity on the beaches. "This would appear to be an opportune time to take a recess ... and Admiral, we look forward to hearing those first reports from the beaches" he said, looking at his watch, "... in the next ten minutes."

~ * ~ * ~ * ~

Seven miles away, approaching the beaches at Livadiya aboard a tank landing craft mechanised, or LCM, another soldier's thoughts were also focussed on the first wave which was minutes from the shore.

Abe Cooper, now a Staff Sergeant in the famed 127th Recon Battalion, stood up in his commander's hatch at the right rear of his light tank, and watched through his field glasses as the two waves of landing craft and amphibious tanks to his front continued resolutely toward land.

Great spouts of white water spewed upwards among the mile-wide formations, from deadly but inaccurate long-range Soviet artillery. The geysers reaching up into the grey sky reminded Cooper of the tornadoes that plagued the midwest every spring. The twisters made him feel just as helpless as he did now – never knowing where they'd touchdown, and nothing you could do about it once they did.

The rocket barrages had ceased several minutes ago, and the lumbering LCIs that had launched them were slowly turning out of formation and heading to the rear. Cooper smiled ruefully at the blazing forest above the beaches, where a vast cloud of smoke was boiling skyward, rising from the flames below.

As the crew below him could not see beyond the closed ramp of the LCM, he shared details of his view with them. "Well guys, I'm sorry to report that we've missed our invitation from the commies to their barbecue ... but it sure looks like some of their kids have been playing with matches."

"Damn," replied Keponee as he sat reading in his gunner's seat on the right-side of the turret. "At least there'll still be a good fire for toasting marshmallows once we land." He flipped a page nonchalantly. Reading a paperback helped to keep his mind off their predicament. Although he was resigned to having their Bulldog confined inside the LCM, he was impatient to get out of their water-taxi and start finding some targets.

Spirits were high aboard the M41A1 Little Bulldog, the latest design of light tank in service with the U.S. Army. The 27th Recon Battalion had been assigned to the 1st Cavalry Division for the landings at Livadiya but would be returned to General Corday's 10th Armoured Division once the beachhead was secure and the rest of 3rd Army had begun to assemble on shore.

"Ten minutes!", a voice blared over the LCM's loudspeakers.

A squadron of fighter bombers launched from the supercarrier United States, roared overhead toward the beach, then climbed above the towering smoke to gain altitude before beginning their attack run. As they diminished into small black specks and reached two thousand feet, Cooper saw ribbons of tracer clawing up from way back in the forest. *AA located,* he thought as he watched the Skyhawks unleash their rockets several miles inland.

Brilliant flashes streaked downwards, striped packets of high velocity destruction which pierced the forest canopy, seeking out the well-camouflaged Soviet artillery that had been firing on the incoming allied landing craft. Cooper couldn't see the result on the ground, nor did he know exactly what the target was, but he watched intently, cheering inside as each plane ascended unscathed through the myriad black puffs of flak that followed them out of their bombing runs.

Could be hitting their heavy artillery ... or armour. We don't know what they might have sitting back there in that forest.

As if to answer his question, the beach itself suddenly erupted with multiple huge blasts. *Shit. That's from some big stuff ... hitting the first wave on the beach.*

He put down his glasses as more waterspouts started creeping their way toward him. "Incoming!" he shouted, warning the crew to close their hatches. The loud slap of a shell hitting the water nearby was followed by a drenching downpour onto the hull of the tank.

Corporal Greene was late closing his driver's hatch so he got a soaking. "Wish they'd take out that damned arty!", he spat with frustration as he began wiping the water away to clear his periscope.

"Ditto" added Keponee in his French-Canadian lilt. "I want to at least fire this seventy-six before we get hit by those poorly trained, pot-luck arty Ivans."

"Trouble is they've got so damn much of it" complained Cooper.

"The commies think artillery will save them the trouble of actually having to fight us once we land," explained Keponee as he patted the breech of the 76mm appreciatively.

"Five minutes!", blared the loudspeaker.

"Right! Cut the chatter ... comms procedure from now on!" barked Cooper.

"Final checks! Prepare to fire." He led the crew through each of the steps. It was the second time they'd been through them since mounting up.

Greene started the engine and then wiped his periscope clean again. Keponee turned the manual safety on the 76mm to the off position. Standing on the left side of the turret, the loader, Trooper Paine, opened and closed the breech to check its readiness for loading.

The crew had drilled these procedures hundreds of times and took only a few seconds to instinctively complete each one. This was the final check before crossing the line of departure and leaving the LCM for the wide-open and shell-torn expanses of the beach.

"Check firing switches; check power control ..." continued Cooper.

Keponee traversed the turret, only slightly to the left and then to the right to avoid striking the sides of the LCM. Then he elevated the gun up and down. All sights were checked and adjusted, and the .50 cals loaded and cocked.

"One minute!"

They could hear the rounds from the Soviet artillery impacting on the beach now only one hundred yards ahead. Being inside the hull of a tank wouldn't protect them from a direct hit, and their armoured enclosure was only making them feel slightly safer than if they were going to be running across the yards of open sand like the Marines and 1st Cavalry troopers were doing.

Cooper cried out the last of the checks, "Report!"

"Gunner ready!"

"Driver ready!"

"Loader ready!"

All four men stared intently through their scopes. There was nothing to see but the bland wall of the ramp's grey steel in front of them. Silent and pensive, they waited, listening to the echo of their own heartbeats throbbing through their arteries and up inside their leather helmets. Outside the tank, the continuous thumping from the barrage kept reminding them of what was waiting for them when that ramp dropped.

"Ten seconds!"

"This is it boys! Live life to the death!" shouted Cooper.

A warning klaxon sounded as the landing craft lunged into shallow water and scraped the sandy bottom. Green revved the 500 HP engine. The ramp fell forward with a splash.

"Go! Go! Go!" screamed Cooper, gripping the handle of the hatch above him for support and the Little Bulldog lurched forward into waist-deep surf.

Greene spotted the cover of trees beyond the beach and accelerated toward them. A shower of wet brown sand burst upward only a few yards away and obscured his view. The blast rocked the light tank and shook up the crew.

"Keep moving! Don't stop until ordered!" urged Cooper. The tank's progress steadied as it moved up the gentle slope of the shore, and he was able to put his eye to his periscope long enough to see what was happening around them. He saw a Marine AmTrac in flames, and the dark shapes of prone, burned bodies lying contrasted against the pale sand around it.

To the eastern side of the three-mile wide bay, Marines from the 5th Marine Division were spilling from their landing craft and following their amphibious tanks up the beach. The enemy artillery fire, although diminishing in intensity as the Allied air strikes began to take their toll, was still sporadic up and down the length of the shoreline, and sprayed deadly shell splinters at the columns of troops behind the armour. Fallen soldiers were immediately picked up by their fellow Marines and carried forward to cover.

The Bulldog rolled on, making headway up the beach, when another shell landed in the deeper, dry sand twenty yards in front of it. The blast was muffled but dumped a thick cloud of sand over the tank, momentarily blocking the crew's periscopes. As the tank's motion helped to move the sand away and unblock the periscopes, Cooper searched the burning coastal vegetation above the beach for targets. The thick smokescreen from the earlier preliminary barrage laid down by the Navy was beginning to dissipate, giving him, and also the enemy, a clearer view of the beach.

"Bunker! Two o'clock, one hundred yards!" he called out.

Keponee followed Cooper's directions and spied the squat concrete shape with a narrow slit across the front. The continuous flashing from the muzzle of the machine gun meant they needed to take it out before any Marines started to die. He started swinging the turret to the left to bring the 76mm gun to bear.

Cooper calmly but urgently gave the orders to engage the target, "Driver halt! Gunner! HE!"

"Up!" replied Paine, immediately confirming that a round of high-explosive was already in the chamber.

"100, MG!", said Cooper calling out the range and target.

"Identified!" said Keponee.

"Fire!"

Keponee pulled the trigger on the hand-grip of the elevation control handle.

"On the way!"

At such close range, a gunner as experienced as Keponee wasn't going to miss. The round punched into the firing slit and detonated. Flame and smoke billowed out from the emplacement, and the machine-gun fell silent. Cooper knew there was little chance of survivors, so he ordered Greene to move on.

The Little Bulldog pushed up into the trees which were either still on fire or just blackened and shattered stumps left behind by the preliminary barrages. Cooper swivelled his scope around. He spotted another bunker, a larger one with two frontal slits, each showing the muzzle flashes from machine-guns. This time he just watched as it was already being assaulted by 1st Cavalry troopers from the first wave.

An eight-man squad was attacking, with covering fire from an LMG. Two soldiers worked their way in close, and let loose with their Browning Automatic Rifles, while a trooper with a bazooka scrambled into firing position. The other four riflemen in the squad were flanking around to make sure no enemy infantry tried to interfere with the assault from either side of the bunker.

The first rocket from the bazooka glanced harmlessly off the outer lip of one of the firing slits and flew into the trees. As the MGs kept pouring their relentless fire onto the troopers down the beach, the bazooka loader tapped the helmet of the operator, and the next rocket went straight through the slit.

A venting exhaust of smoke and dust coincided with a hollow thump, and one of the MGs stopped firing. Cooper then lost sight of the remainder of the assault as the Bulldog pushed deeper into the burning, smoking and ashened remains of the undergrowth.

Some of the surviving communist artillery, under orders from observers concealed in the vicinity of the bay, now shifted their fire further inland as the Allies pushed up from the shore. At the same time, the Soviet infantry who were being routed by the advancing 1st Cavalry and Marines, were leaving their weapon pits and bunkers and beginning to retreat through the scorched and splintered posts which had once been trees.

Huh … so no fight to the death from these sons of bitches, thought Cooper, watching through his scope as several enemy rounds exploded and cut down some of their own men. Disgusted, he pressed the override lever on his power control handle and took control of the turret. This also gave him control of the coaxial machine-gun. Once on target, he pulled the firing trigger and the .30 cal pounded out its beat of destruction. Two hundred yards away, pillars of dirt kicked up among the fleeing reds. Cooper's dispassionate eyes moved their intense focus from one moving target to the next as the rounds bit into wood, soil and flesh, spraying blood, splinters and gusts of black ash into the air.

It had been almost two years since he'd felt that same cold indifference to human life – and as he kept on firing, thoughts of his dead brother helped fuel his lust for killing. He fired at the communists until the MG's ammo belt was empty.

While Paine reloaded, Cooper squashed any feelings of remorse other soldiers might have felt. *Insects. You chose to serve your party and the party says the state is everything and the individual is nothing … well now you're getting paid for your service.*

His anger rose as he scanned around and saw an AmTrac get hit nearby, slewing to one side as a broken track peeled off its rollers. An unseen Soviet anti-tank gun had been moved up to cover the retreat, and the US ground troops immediately went into action to locate and take it out.

Aware of his own tank's vulnerability, Cooper ordered Greene to leave the area. "Driver get us out of here!" he bellowed urgently. "We've done our job … move us back out and then head over to the west to the battalion rally point."

As they threaded their back way through the overrun enemy defences, Cooper had a moment to reflect on his brother. It struck him that he'd not thought about him in the days leading up to the landing. *Guess I blocked him out,* he thought with a pang of guilt. *After he lost his arm hitting the beach at Gdansk … guess I thought the same thing might happen to me.*

He choked down the lump in his throat. This wasn't the time for him to be lamenting his loss, but having just taken out his vengeance on the same Soviet communists who were responsible for Aaron's death had reopened an old wound.

Goddam useless doctors … why couldn't they save him?

He remembered hearing the news while he'd been on a training exercise in Japan. Aaron had been fine before an infection had finally taken hold and the blood poisoning got him.

Fucking commies.

Once they were away from the fighting, Cooper looked around for the other Bulldogs from his troop. Their orders had been to get off the beach using their own initiative. It was a tactic which would allow for any mishaps such as their LCMs dropping them off at the wrong locations. Once landed, they had been tasked with fighting alongside the 1st Cavalry to secure the beachheads on the headland, and then regroup before heading west from Livadiya along the road which crossed the top of the headland and led to Abrek Bay three miles away.

It was toward Abrek that the 1st Cavalry Division would be pushing once Livadaya, and Trudny Peninsula where the 1st and 3rd Marine Divisions had landed to the east, had been cleared of the enemy. The Bulldogs were to scout for a

Marine task force formed specifically for the spearhead operation as it moved toward Abrek, in an effort to secure the left flank of the Trudny beachheads.

As leader, Cooper got on the radio and requested a sitrep from each of the four other light tanks in his troop. All but one were still operational, with the other having been disabled by an anti-tank mine.

As he clicked off the mic, the deafening roar of fighter-bombers overhead caused him to look up. Dozens of Skyraiders and Corsairs screamed in low, heading toward the heavily forested interior. As they passed over, Cooper could make out the glint of silver way up through the clouds. Flying at a much higher altitude, a flight of B29 Superfortresses were heading deeper inland.

The B29s would have been timed to arrive at the Russian coast after leaving their airstrips in Japan two hours earlier. Cooper imagined the destruction awaiting the Soviets, with each bomber carrying a twenty-thousand pound payload.

As the Bulldog motored through the blackened landscape, it was eventually joined by the three other tanks in the troop. The Soviet artillery had subsided to a point where the Nakhodka beachheads were declared secure, and now the massive LST landing ships were sliding up to the shore. Even a veteran such as Cooper couldn't help but be impressed as the huge bow doors on the front of one of the ships yawed wide open, and a ramp deployed from within. Moments later, the first of the 10th Armoured Division's T32 Grizzly and T30 Mammoth heavy tanks rolled out on to the sand.

A second LST ground its way ashore, combat-loaded so that the most vital equipment could be unloaded first. In this case, it was a bulldozer. Each LST was carrying two-thousand tons of ordnance, and another two hundred of those ships were milling around out to sea, waiting for their turn to come in and unload.

Cooper's troop pushed on past the western side of Trudny Peninsula, in the direction of Abrek Bay. Due to the confined access to Abrek caused by Putyatin island blocking the approaches from the sea, the possibility of any landings there were unlikely and so it would be relatively undefended.

A reconnaissance in-force by a Marine Regimental Combat Team who would move out from the landing zone toward the west, was intended to eventually protect the entire left flank of the landings. Offshore from Abrek Bay, Putyatin Island had been taken by an airborne operation during the night, and once Abrek Bay was secured by the 3rd Marine Division RCT, then the offensive push inland from the main landings could proceed with more confidence.

The RCT also included a battalion of heavy artillery and a battalion of 1st Cavalry Combat Engineers who would clear any mines and other obstacles along the way. Cooper's troop, along with another 27th Recon light tank unit, joined the RCT at the western end of the Livadiya landing beaches. The Little Bulldogs had been selected for the mission because they had increased fire-power and thicker armour compared to the M24 Chaffees still in service with the Marine Corps. A Marine RCT had been selected for the spearhead operation due to the lightweight and highly mobile nature of Marine formations. As opposed to regular infantry or armoured divisions, they were organised to be highly coordinated and self-contained, so their units could reform quickly for operations such this one. Although an arm of the US Navy, the Marine Corps also had their own Marine Air Wing, armour and artillery units, so they had evolved into a true rapid-response military force.

Cooper checked in with the Marine Colonel commanding the RCT and then ensured his crew got a few hours rest before they would have to move off again. At 0400 HRS the next day, Buster's troop went on ahead as light tanks always do, leaving Livadiya behind, and striking out for the coastal road which led toward Abrek Bay.

Later that morning on the USS Salem, General MacArthur's major concern now that the beachheads were secure, was not what the Soviets were now going to do. He thought it was unlikely they would counter-attack in strength here, as most of their divisions were engaged with Vlasov's army to the north, or else deployed on Muravyov-Amursky Peninsula across the gulf from the Allied landings for the defence of Vladivostok.

No ... he thought grimly as he stepped back from the huddle of officers at the conference table ... *there's a much graver issue pending. Now that the Union of Nations has played its hand here, the question is ... will the Chinese intervene?*

CHAPTER TWENTY-SEVEN

"Power grows out of the barrel of a gun"
Mao Zedong

CCP House of Reception,
Peking, China
July 1ˢᵗ, 1949 1100 HRS

Josef Stalin took the same seat in the anteroom in which he'd presented Mao with the designs for the atom bomb.

This time he was accompanied by more than just his aide and an interpreter. Several high-ranking generals and the commander of the armies of the Far Eastern Soviet, Marshal Meretskov, were with him for this crucial meeting. The former Russians all sat on one side of the long conference table, waiting for the arrival of the Chinese delegation under the watchful gaze of soldiers from the CCP's Red Guard lined up along the opposite wall.

A CCP official stood by the main door, making no effort to disguise the contempt in his narrowed eyes. A frustrated Stalin leant to his left and spoke quietly to Meretskov, "This is typical of the Chinese. They make us wait here to exemplify their position of having power over us. It is the legacy of Mao's paranoia. Be sure your generals continue their conversations, and absolutely do not show any impatience or discomfort."

Stalin looked to his side and viewed the row of Soviet officers with satisfaction. Their uniforms brimmed with gold stars mounted on red epaulettes, and he felt more empowered than the last time he'd sat at this table. He was struck by the irony that although on his last visit he'd brought the Chinese a weapon of mass destruction, he was now in an even stronger bargaining position to prevent the reluctant CCP from remaining isolated from the escalating conflict in the Russian Far East. His years spent fighting his way to the top of the Bolshevik party had taught him patience ... and tact. Although he had given the Chinese the plans for an A-bomb, he had one more bargaining chip at his disposal, and following the Union of Nations invasion of Soviet territory, he knew that now was the time to use it.

Ten minutes passed. A Chinese attendant filled the empty glasses in front of the waiting Soviet generals with water, and then went to fill Stalin's. Stalin put his hand over the empty glass while glancing at the CCP official by the door to ensure that he noticed that the leader of the visiting Soviets was not partaking of any of the provided refreshment. It seemed to be a cue, as the CCP official tapped on the door which presently opened part way, and a few words were spoken through the gap.

The unconcern of a bully used to getting his own way relaxed Stalin's bearing as he continued to converse with Meretskov. Another five minutes passed before the door finally opened and Mao entered, followed by Zhou Enlai and an entourage of military staff.

Without looking at Stalin, the Chinese leader sat down at the head of the table with his interpreter beside him. He then spoke to those gathered around the table as one, "Comrades, the business we are about to conduct here will have a singular purpose; to affirm the position of the People's Republic of China with regard to the security of its northern border, and to reiterate that any plea for intervention following the Allied invasion there yesterday will only be considered with the benefit of the Chinese nation in mind."

He turned his gaze in Stalin's direction, "Prime Minister, you may address your plea to my own Prime Minister, Zhou Enlai."

Stalin's eyes narrowed. He had expected the Chinese to be recalcitrant, but Mao's opening had taken him by surprise with its blatant lack of diplomacy. It was as though the CCP were downplaying his role as the leader of the Russian communists. He looked across the table at Zhou who was dressed in a bland grey suit matching those of his compatriots instead of the stylish formal dress he had usually been known for when he had been Foreign Minister.

"Prime Minister," Stalin said sternly, "The Far Eastern Soviet does not *plea* for assistance. Nor do we wish to let the People's Republic of China continue under the misapprehension that the attack on our territory is solely directed at ourselves."

He leant forward and helped himself to a glass of water. As he took a long slow drink, he could feel the cold glares of the Chinese upon him. He held up the glass, now half empty, and continued, "Water. As essential to our existence as the air we are all breathing, or the produce of the soil we all consume – our agriculture."

He put the glass down, "We have followed with interest, the progress of your country's efforts to collectivise the hundreds of thousands of your villages, and to integrate their agricultural practices into the overall direction of your Party."

He let out a grim chuckle, "To say that the results so far are as *effective* as those we saw in the Soviet Union would be an understatement." He focussed on Mao who was a statue of indifference with an unreadable expression.

"The widespread famine currently devastating your country should serve as a warning!" he exclaimed. "The same interference from foreign capitalists which subverted our own attempts to unify the people, is clearly at work in disrupting your own country's long march to freedom."

Mao stared down the centre of the table, appearing to be devoid of any emotion, or conscience. Millions of his people were starving, but all the Party members at the table looked very well fed.

Stalin switched his attention back to Zhou, "Prime Minister, what is now occurring in your country is a repeat of the events in the Soviet Union. Our revolution to raise the proletariat from its servitude and cleanse society of the bourgeois capitalists was thwarted by an international conspiracy aimed at destroying socialism. We now see that the same forces from the West are invading our Far Eastern Soviet ... and do not fool yourselves! They will not stop there!"

Zhou looked searchingly to the head of the table where Mao sat with his hands clasped resting on the table. The CCP leader sighed, placing his palms flat down in front of him as though he were suppressing any resistance to his will from those he was addressing. "Minister Stalin," he said in a condescending tone, "China's victorious struggle has been far more efficient in eliminating the reactionaries and criminal classes from our society than the insipid attempt by the Soviet Union. A people's revolution requires at its source, a committed and ruthless population. The masses accuse and then prosecute the criminal landowners, and they also execute the sentence ... which must always be death."

Stalin was imitating his host by staring straight ahead as Mao continued. "The same masses will defend to their last breath, what they have fought for so long to achieve. We have no fear of these international forces you speak of."

Stalin's stare dropped to his own hands as he shrugged off the insult to failed Russian communism. After a moment, he lifted his head, looking Mao straight in the eye, and stated with grave conviction, "Chairman ... if you allow the West to prevail on your borders they will be encouraged to complete their mission of ridding the world of communist ideals. They have unlimited material resources and productive capacity at their disposal. The designs for military equipment I provided you, although superior to those of the Allies, will not maintain your advantage for long. The westerners will be continually improving their weaponry to match yours!"

The frustration stemming from Stalin's humiliation boiled over to anger.

"You must strike now!" he cried as his fist slammed into the table.

Mao flinched at the outburst, then levelled a hostile gaze at Stalin, "We will act as we see fit! The world will not see us as the aggressor!"

"The world? What do we care what the world thinks!!" shouted Stalin, then he snorted with derision, "The world will soon be controlled by the Union of Nations ... that collection of criminals who are suffering the delusion that individuals are more important than the governments that lead them." The pitch of his voice changed from that of a warning to a more sinister threat, "Once we have enough uranium to build a hundred A-bombs the world will have to negotiate a peace ... and it will be on our terms."

Mao shook his head, sneering grudgingly, but still admiring his counterpart's bravado. "Yes, I am sure this could be so comrade. But first we have to obtain that uranium, and that could take us years."

The Chairman looked to his Prime Minister for confirmation. Zhou leafed through his notes and after flipping a few pages he read aloud, "The RBMK reactor being built at Xianyang will not be producing weapons-grade uranium 235 for another eighteen months. We are actively searching for sources of raw uranium for the enrichment process."

"You see?" said Mao, "It will be too late for us to be in a position to threaten them with this weapon."

Stalin chuckled, enjoying the moment. It was time to play his final card. Like a drug dealer who had gotten his victim to come back for another hit of cocaine, now it was time to supply him with the heroin. He nodded to his aide. The Soviet officer carefully retrieved a small lead-lined box from his attaché case and placed it on the table. He opened it and then passed the contents to his boss. Stalin held up the vial and tapped it gently with his stubby finger. Inside it, a slug of uranium 235 emitted a small dose of its lethal radiation.

"This is but a tiny sample from the sixty kilograms of weapons-grade uranium 235 we have acquired. This last gift to you will complete what you need."

"But how?" asked Mao with astonishment.

"Once again, we still have many comrades in Russia; some with access to the resources the Soviet Union obtained from the Nazis. The Germans had been stock-piling uranium for years, much of which the Soviet Union seized and used to supply a prototype reactor in the Ural Mountains. All of this time that we have been resisting Vlasov's armies, we also managed to infiltrate that plant and recover a large quantity of the enriched uranium produced there."

"How much is needed for a bomb?" asked Mao.

"There is enough for a single weapon. The same weapon for which you already possess the designs. All we ask in return is for you to intervene in the Allied invasion of our territory."

He rolled the vial along the table to Mao. The Chinese leader looked at it for a moment before reluctantly picking it up.

"It appears that our destinies will coincide after all ... and that we are on a path to unleash a monster of sufficient strength to battle that of the westerners."

A dark foreboding greyed Mao's expression, "Prime Minister Stalin, you will be aided by the might of our People's Liberation Army; its powerful arsenal – and its endless supply of soldiers who are willing to die for the cause of global communism."

Mao looked around the table, "Comrades! As we continue our great struggle to spread the socialist ideal to every other country in this world, we will recognise the contribution made by the Soviet Union. The ideals spawned by Marx, and so effectively implemented by Lenin and the Bolsheviks, have been a source of inspiration for the rise of communism in China."

We share the same goals – to see the Communist Party at the head of every nation on Earth. To see every man, woman and child labouring for the same singular purpose – to serve the Party!"

He focussed on Stalin, "Now, our comrades need our help to take back the revolution that the capitalist reactionaries stole from them. China – not Russia, will lead the inevitable march to bring all of humanity into the Party's glorious embrace!"

CHAPTER TWENTY-EIGHT

Abrek Bay,
Russian Far East
July 1st, 1949 1330 HRS

The Marine RCT supported by 1st Cavalry's Bulldogs had made solid progress since leaving the beach at Livadiya in the early hours. They were moving as fast as the terrain would allow, with the Marine commander pushing his units forward constantly. They had a deadline to meet because the longer it took to secure the left flank of the landings, the more time the Soviets would have to send reinforcements from Vladivostok down the road that ran along the coastline to the Allied beachhead. To protect the landings, that road from the north-west had to be denied to the Soviets. It was the RCT's job to ensure that Abrek Bay and the road above it were both secured.

At the same time, the RCT would be moving as fast as possible to make sure any retreating Soviets did not have time to regroup and organise any significant defences ahead of it.

Having reached the headland separating Trudny Peninsula from Abrek Bay, 1st Cavalry's light tanks were now spread out on either side of a dirt road. Their role was one of exposing any enemy positions that may be covering the road, and to provide fire support if any roadblocks were encountered.

The countryside was covered by dense coastal brush which limited visibility, and the tanks were relying on the

Marines accompanying them to thwart any attacks from concealed enemy anti-tank guns or infantry AT weapons.

Standing up in his commander's hatch with his field glasses, Staff Sergeant Cooper scanned the forward 180 degrees constantly as they tracked through the undergrowth to the left of the road. Stunted trees and thick shrubs were crushed and flattened by the twenty-six ton tank as it moved forward at only five miles per hour.

Cooper hated being restricted to such a slow pace. He recalled the words of his instructor at the tank school, "Anti-tank weapons lack the traverse and optical sighting mechanism to track fast moving targets."

He sighed at the memory made distant by the intervening years of war. It was those words which had helped build an aura of invulnerability around he and his crew's tank, and had been the logic behind their motto of 'speed, swerve and smoke'. That motto evolved into the name that had adorned Three-Z, the Chaffee that had served them so well in Europe, but after Three-Z's destruction, Cooper had felt some of the invulnerability fade. *I sure am not feeling invulnerable right now doing just 5mph through ideal ambush country.*

He patted the side of the turret where the name of their new tank was now painted, "Buster". *We just gotta hope this little bulldog has enough armour and firepower so she doesn't need to be doin' the three Z's.*

He spotted a likely site for concealing an enemy position up ahead.

"Kep, keep your eyes on that thicket of trees at ten o'clock" advised Cooper.

"Roger," replied the gunner as he swung the turret fifteen degrees to the left.

The Marines trotting behind the tank saw where the snout of the Bulldog's 76mm gun had shifted to, and their platoon leader signalled for one of his squads to flank out to the left and reconnoitre the two hundred yards of ground between them and the thicket.

The advance from Nakhodka on Trudny Peninsula was also proceeding at a fast pace. The continuous sounds of battle resonated from miles inland and from the naval gunfire offshore as those first divisions to land now pushed outward to the north toward Nikolayevka, and also to follow the coast road behind the 1st Cavalry to their east.

Nearer to Cooper's Bulldog, a series of explosions boomed out from the direction of the dirt road one hundred yards to their right. The crew ignored the blasts as they'd become used to the frequent sounds of enemy anti-tank mines being detonated by the RCT's engineers as they cleared the road.

Cooper called for Greene to bring Buster to a halt while the Marines flanking left drew closer to the stand of trees. The Soviets were experts at camouflaging their positions, and Cooper was reminded of their efforts around the Bialystok salient in 1946 which had so very effectively hidden the extensive fortifications there.

Don't think we'll come across anything like that here but we may do once we get further inland.

The Marines soon signalled the all-clear from the flank and Cooper ordered Greene to move off again. The Bulldog's engine growled and Keponee swung the turret back to twelve o'clock, easing his finger off the firing lever. He was in his element. *Just like stalking elk in the Rockies only not so quiet,* he thought, relishing the surrounds as though it were he that were concealed from his prey, and the Soviets were sitting in the bush just waiting to be picked off by the destructive power of his mighty 76mm gun.

Another hundred yards of crashing through the brush and the Bulldog suddenly found itself breaking out of the trees and into a wide clearing. Cooper thought there was something unnatural about it, as it extended all the way to the road, providing the opposite side with a clear field of fire onto any vehicles traversing it. He inspected the ground below which appeared to have been scorched some time ago. Alarm bells rang inside his head and he immediately barked out orders.

"Driver back up!" he shouted as he noticed a movement straight across the other side of the clearing. As the tank began to reverse, Cooper instinctively knew that anything in front of them was hostile.

"Gunner! Battle sight! Infantry! Fire!"

The battle sight command meant that the target was at a predetermined range and heading and Keponee just had to instantly fire the loaded HE round. The 76mm barked and the greenery across the other side erupted in a ball of flame and debris. Cooper let rip with the .50 cal just as he saw a flash and then a projectile streaking toward them.

"RPG!"

Buster had gathered enough rearward momentum for the rocket to sail past inches in front of the tank. It exploded against a tree, spraying splinters at the Marines near the tank who had spread out and ducked, and were now crouching around the edge of the clearing.

As Cooper kept firing the machine gun, Keponee adjusted fire to where the tracer rounds were going, and Paine loaded another round of HE and slammed the breech closed.

"Up!" he cried.

A split second later Keponee saw the gun-ready light come on, put his eye over the gunsight eyepiece and then pulled the fire lever.

At the same time another RPG lanced over the flat expanse and struck one of the other Bulldogs that had just emerged from the trees. The tank's track was hit and it rocked to a halt.

Buster rolled backwards into the trees and Cooper ducked down into the turret, narrowly missing being clouted by an overhanging branch. The branch struck the .50 cal, spinning it around on its mounting. Leaves and foliage showered down onto Cooper through the open hatch.

"Driver halt!" he ordered, and put his eye up to his periscope. The view was blocked, so he reached out through the opening to clear the cupola's view ports. Bullets were clanging against the hull from enemy machine guns, and from all around the tanks the sound of rifles, BARs and LMGs opened up as the Marines hugged the ground and returned fire.

With his view of the enemy obscured by the trees, Keponee decided he would be wasting rounds using the main gun, so he switched to firing the co-axial .30 cal mounted next to the 76mm. As he pulled the trigger on the hand-grip with his left hand, he slowly used his right hand to traverse the turret.

The machine gun's rounds pumped into the brush on the opposite side of the clearing, keeping the Soviet's heads down. By now, Cooper had removed the leaves and small branches covering his viewports, but still couldn't see clearly ahead of him through the tree's branches. Deciding that the enemy also wouldn't have a clear shot, he stood up in his cupola and took up the .50 cal again.

He had to turn his head to one side as he started firing as the splinters from the shattered branches in front of the machine gun flew back toward him. Within seconds an opening in the foliage formed through which he could see the flashes of the enemy small arms.

The sound of the heavy MG firing up again was music to the ears of the Marines, and the boom-boom-booming retort echoed across the clearing like a racing heartbeat. The most feared anti-infantry weapon on the battlefield started killing and maiming any of the unseen enemy who tried to raise their heads from out of their weapon pits to fire back.

A Soviet soldier with an RPG left cover and tried to get a shot on the disabled Bulldog. Cooper spotted him and swung his gun around. As the bullets punched through the enemy soldier, blood and limbs flew into the air from the dismembered torso.

Cooper felt no sympathy, only the hate-fuelled bloodlust which made the memories of his dead brother more bearable.

The Soviet MGs were still laying down a murderous fusillade across the open spaces in front of the grounded company of Marines. The company's captain decided not to risk any of his men by assaulting the communist gun emplacements directly, so he radioed the RCT's artillery battalion and called for fire support.

Within a minute, the first of the 155mm salvoes arrived and began to extinguish all life inside the radius of the coordinates provided by the Marine Captain. With complete air-superiority over the entire region of the landings, the Union of Nations forces could deploy all of their overwhelming firepower wherever they chose. Any enemy artillery which responded would quickly be detected and destroyed by either air-strikes, naval gunfire or a counter-barrage from the steadily increasing number of artillery battalions arriving on the beaches.

After correcting the first salvo, the Marine captain watched with satisfaction as each of the massive blasts blew tons of earth skyward, gouging great holes in the ground and spewing trees, dirt and human debris into the air.

The Captain's impassivity was sourced from a different place to that of Staff Sergeant Cooper. His stemmed from the knowledge that he was saving the lives of his men.

Nowhere along the three-hundred yard frontage of the opposite side of the clearing was spared from the concentrated barrage from all four batteries of the artillery battalion. The enemy activity soon diminished, and the allied soldiers ceased fire. Fifteen minutes later the barrage stopped and the Marines sent out flanking patrols to probe the Soviet positions. Cooper and his crew waited while a company of combat engineers from 1st Cavalry followed up on the Marines and cleared along the roadside to their right of any mines not already detonated by the barrage.

It was now late afternoon and Cooper was aware that the RCT needed to cross the remaining two miles to Abrek Bay before dark.

The Marines patrols encountered only light resistance which was soon mopped up. The RCT got rolling again, and by 1700 HRS following minor delays from mines and repairing damage to the road, had reached its objective.

Due to the unsuitability of Abrek Bay for any landings, the Soviets had no significant fortifications there. The light tanks quickly skirted above the beach accompanied by engineers and Marine units mounted in half-tracks to secure the area. A pair of bunkers, one at each end of the bay, were facing the sea, and so provided no opposition to the Marines attacking from behind.

Once Abrek had been taken, Buster halted on a low promontory overlooking the western end of the bay, and the crew dismounted. The previously overcast sky had now cleared following the freshening of an onshore wind, and the salt air was a tonic for the crew after so many hours spent inside the pungent confines of the tank.

Finally allowed a reprieve after two days of fighting, Staff Sergeant Cooper made sure his crew were given time to recover, both physically and mentally.

The combat fatigue brought on from hour after hour of extreme stress required the body and mind to have time to deal with what they had just been through. The veterans knew how to wind down, but Cooper paid special attention to Trooper Paine after his first taste of war.

"Paine, how're goin'? Get a headache from that shitshow?" asked Cooper as he sat reclining with his back against one of Buster's road wheels, tossing a baseball up and down in one hand.

"Nah Sarge...I'm holdin' up ok," replied the loader.

As the youngest and newest addition to Buster, the months he'd spent with the others during training exercises in Japan meant that he'd slotted straight in to the tight-knit functioning of a veteran tank crew. The years of experience of those veterans, and their cool heads under fire, had given Paine the confidence to keep his fear in check, and to keep the guns loaded without any mishaps.

They all sat or lay around on the ground, eating C-rations and watching the Marines and engineers as they began setting up a defensive perimeter.

Cooper caught the ball and held it up in front of him. The writing on it was faded, but he could still make out the scrawled signature from Babe Ruth. Even though he wasn't a Yankees fan, his brother had got it signed when he was a kid during one of Ruth's barnstorming tours in the thirties. They'd thrown it to each other all the time, but never used it for batting practice.

He shoved it back in his jacket pocket and closed his eyes, letting the sunshine on his face draw out some of his own stress and strain.

"Hey Sarge, do we get a day off now to go to the beach?" asked Paine.

Mentally exhausted and stinking of sweat, the rookie stared out at the waters of the bay, "It's probably cold but I could sure do with a swim anyway."

"In the sea?" said Keponee incredulously, "Are you fucking crazy? Do you know how dangerous it is to go swimming down there ... crabs, jellyfish ... and *sharks*! Geez man – give me a fair chance in a tank against hordes of Reds any day before I go out in that shit!"

Mojave Sentinel
Union of Nations Science Foundation (UNSCIF) Research
Station
Antarctica
July 4th, 2246 CE

The UNSCIF Chief Scientist, Professor Abel Biselki, announced to a press conference today, that an international team of physicists from the Quantum Optic Research Laboratory (QORL) had successfully transported an object using a quantum carrier light-wave.

The object, a grain of molybdenum, was moved a distance of ten metres along a specially built chamber. The facility's 20 mega-watt laser has been constructed underground, enclosed by Antarctica's deep ice pack, to assist with the extreme cooling requirements for the experiments.

The team's research paper states that their technology, based on the principles of quantum tunnelling, enabled the object to be 'temporarily shifted into an inter-dimensional state' and that they have named this region 'Null Space'.

Prof. Biselki said that the technology developed by QORL is now at the forefront of UNSCIF's research programs with intended applications for interstellar, or possibly even intergalactic travel.

CHAPTER TWENTY-NINE

*"No beast so fierce but knows some touch of pity, but I
know none, and therefore am no beast."*
William Shakespeare

Bol'shoy Kamen,
Russian Far East
July 9th, 1949

Windswept salt air mixing with the light patter of rain elevated General MacArthur's spirits. The seemingly endless hours spent in secluded conferences and planning sessions had been wearing away at him. His thoughts were constantly of his soldiers out in the field, exposed to the elements and fighting for their lives – and ultimately for their way of life.

From under the cover of trees fringing the rocky coast of Ussuri Bay, he watched a massive pall of grey smoke rise resolutely from Vladivostok, ten miles away on the other side of the bay. Visibility across the water was poor, and it looked as though the boiling grey column trying to force its way upwards was being pushed back down by the even darker grey sheets of rain from above.

As the Seventh Fleet continued its bombardment of the defences around the city, a low-pressure system had arrived from the Sea of Japan and was delivering an early summer deluge onto whole of the Primorsky Krai region, bringing a temporary halt to MacArthur's tour of the front lines.

"How are your roads holding up General?" he asked the tall, charismatic figure standing beside him.

General Patton lowered his field glasses, disappointed that the weather had denied him a better view of the Soviet-held city which was soon to be cut off from its main army in the north. "We've got six battalions of engineers, plus the Navy Seabees, working round the clock to build new ones and keep the existing ones open," he advised. "They now have a bunch of quarries in production supplying aggregate, and more will soon be unloading from the beaches."

He looked despondently upwards at the dismal grey sky, "The sooner this damn rain moves inland the better they'll be able to work on the key route leading westward across from Nikolayevka ... it's at risk from flooding where it runs along the Partizanskaya River."

MacArthur gave no clue to the concerns he was feeling. The condition of the roads was critical to enabling 3rd Army to move forward rapidly and trap as many of the Soviets around Vladivostok as possible. He spoke to the General of the Army with a detached calm, knowing that as overall commander of ground forces in the Russian Far East, Patton didn't need any micro-management. "I expect General Walker will be on top of that situation." He gave Patton a wry grin, "And I'm sure you'll have no regrets about your decision to put him in command of your precious 3rd Army."

Patton detected the hint of cunning in MacArthur's tone, knowing that the Supreme Commander had some doubts about Walker. Having personal experience with Walker as one of his Corps commanders during the fighting in Europe, Patton had no doubts about the fellow West Pointer from Texas.

"Walker's the right man for the job. We need someone dependable that won't flinch when asked to do the tough jobs – one that doesn't use too much imagination or take too many risks to get them done."

MacArthur said nothing further and went back to viewing the opposite coast. The two generals had adjusted their schedules so they could have this meeting. Patton had been on his way to see General Walker, and MacArthur had just left a press conference giving an update on the overall progress of the Allied advance from the landing beaches. To the group of staff officers behind them, the sight of the two iconic military figures standing side by side was an inspiration, and a poignant warning to the enemy, of the unmistakeable intent of the Union of Nations to bring a timely end to the conflict in Russia.

With the beachheads at Nakhodka established and troops and materiel pouring ashore, MacArthur had called on Patton to form up Walker's 3rd Army for the assault on Vladivostok. The other US army under Patton's command, 1st Army, would be following up once the port at Vladivostok had been taken. As the entire Russian Far East theatre was now under the direction of the Union of Nations Security Council, Patton was also responsible for the Russian armies fighting to the north, but due to the immediate situation on the coast, he was yet to meet directly with their Russian commanders.

MacArthur turned and looked back to the east, toward the bombed-out port of Bol'shoy Kamen. The retreating communists had destroyed the facilities to deny them to the Allies, but the effort had been unnecessary due to the port being only ten miles across the bay from Vladivostok and was within range of the larger calibre Soviet artillery there. Several ships, mostly small freighters, had been sunk by UoN air attacks on the first day of Operation Freehand. Their broken hulks were jutting out of the water as though they were frozen in the last desperate, clamouring moment to gain a breath before being dragged beneath the surface of the harbour.

MacArthur had seen hundreds of such scenes of destruction during his march across the Pacific against the Japanese only a handful of years before, yet here he was once again. Another war, against another fanatical enemy, but for a wholly different purpose. The Union of Nations, according to its Charter, had resolved to aid the Russian democracy led by President Vlasov, and to assist them in the removal of the threat posed by the communists to peace throughout the region. The Soviet army, comprised of Bolsheviks and many former Red Army hard-liners and NKVD regulars, numbered over three hundred thousand.

Patton stepped around beside MacArthur and raised his glasses to view beyond the port, toward the north. Always respecting the resourcefulness of his enemies, he considered for a moment the possibility that they might attempt an amphibious assault here, to try to disrupt the Allied supply lines. He immediately squashed the thought, as he knew that the communists did not possess the craft required to mount such an operation, nor could one survive beneath the total air supremacy currently held by the Allies. As his view drifted farther afield, his thoughts of possible enemy intentions also expanded, and he probed MacArthur for his opinion. "What likelihood is there of the Chinese escalating their involvement?"

They'd already discussed the situation where the Chinese were known to be supplying the Soviets with significant amounts of armaments. Until now, those had been arriving by sea, but that route was no longer available now that Allied fleets controlled the entire northern Pacific. That meant that the Chinese arms would all be coming across the border by road or via the rail link through Suifenho. If they were bringing in supplies by land, they could also be considering bringing in their own troops.

MacArthur shrugged, "The Chinese do not worry me. I have no fear of them intervening in a more direct manner. As far as I'm concerned it would be advantageous to us."

He noticed Patton's look of surprise and knowing he may not be as well informed on the political situation, decided to elaborate to spare him any speculation on his motives. "Washington ... for all its recalcitrance and muddling attempts to handcuff our efforts here, still realises that under the auspices of the UoN Charter we are engaged in an effort that seeks not just to assist the Russian people in ending their civil war, but to continue a much wider conflict." He gave Patton a knowing look, "This is a continuation of the same conflict we fought to free Europe from the Soviets in Moscow. I also see it as one that will inevitably spread throughout the Far East." He fixed his gaze on Patton to confirm that his top field commander understood the significance of his words. "The Union of Nations provides the international framework that every country needs for them to adopt a constitution that will ensure that their people can live under an umbrella of popular democracy, and basic human rights such as personal liberty and equality."

The two generals turned back toward the smoking ruin of Vladivostok and MacArthur continued, "I see this war as an all-encompassing conflict to finally unify humanity. The communists in China will merely see it as a threat to their hold on power ... an attempt to break the stranglehold they inflict upon their own people."

"I agree," said Patton, "... and that's the real tragedy here. Those poor bastards don't even realise how enslaved they are."

MacArthur nodded, "Yes, I'm afraid the weak-minded are easily deceived." He straightened, stretching his tall, angular frame as though he'd completed the surveying of this area of the war he was overseeing, and was ready to move on to the next. He considered the man standing beside him and reflected on the opinion of Patton he'd held in previous years.

"George, I know in the past that it's been reported that you would not be welcome in a role under my command."

The two veteran warriors stood gazing out over the waters of Ussuri Bay, not looking at each other as MacArthur explained himself. "I'd like you to know that I was influenced as much as any other man by the popular press, which painted you as an egotist, and that your victories were motivated by vanity. But knowing you personally as I do now, I can assure you that I recognise my error, and that your command of the Allied ground forces in Russia will be received with the highest confidence and deserve nothing but my fullest support."

He gave Patton a sideways glance, quoting Shakespeare as he often did, "I have no spur to prick the sides of my intent, but only vaulting ambition, which o'erleaps itself and falls on the other."

Patton was moved by MacArthur's admission, "Thank you Douglas. You know ... I earnestly believe that we are both here to fulfil a divine purpose," he said humbly. "Like myself, you've brushed aside death many times ... perhaps with God's help, or merely from the courage gained by the certainty of our faith."

He pointed the cane he usually carried with him when touring the front lines to the north, in the direction his armies would be heading to destroy the last of the Soviet forces. "I sincerely believe that I have survived those many encounters with death so that I can continue on my path toward a greater destiny. It's a destiny I'm sure we both share, and one that meets God's purpose – as you said, a purpose that will unify humanity."

MacArthur, also a man of faith, tipped his peaked cap at the great General, acknowledging that Patton's thoughts on the hand of Providence coincided with his own. With that, the two leaders concluded their meeting and left the coastline to continue on their separate journeys.

CHAPTER THIRTY

Nagqu River,
Nagqu County,
200 miles from Lhasa, Tibet
July 10th, 1949

The forest and scrub on either side of the Nagqu River was on fire. In a last-ditch attempt to thwart a crossing by the Chinese, the Tibetans had laid down a barrage of incendiaries. A widespread blanket of smoke streaked with orange flame rose from the river valley, stretching for thousands of feet into the otherwise clear blue sky. It was a harrowing monument to the Tibetan's failing struggle. One that could be seen by its people from many miles away.

From the fading light of dusk, Colonel Blackett walked into the torch-lit gloom of his command post. The CP was just an earthen dugout with walls lined by wooden logs. The roof was also timber, covered by a thick layer of soil, but the protection it provided was more mental than physical, as a direct hit from artillery would leave no survivors.

His staff together with Lobsang and some of the other Khampa chiefs were already waiting for him, sitting on stumps or standing around the map table. Lieutenant Phuntsok lifted himself up wearily from his seat on one of the cut lengths of tree trunk, but Blackett waved for him to sit back down. "At ease ... this won't take long."

The CIG Colonel cast a quick glance over the map of the local area, noting where the red markers had been moved over from the opposite side of the river. "Well ..." he began disconsolately, "The fires are slowing them down, but we'll have to start our withdrawal in the morning."

He looked at Rhuzkoi, who was now in command of a company of Tibetan Army regulars who had been trickling in from the east over the previous weeks. The Tibetan soldiers had brought with them stories of the atrocities being committed upon the local inhabitants by the communists on their march from Chamdo toward Lhasa. Monasteries were being destroyed and the monks terrorised and tortured.

"Colonel Rhuzkoi, I'll need your men to provide a rearguard at first light in the morning."

"Da, certainly. They are all ready to fight again," he replied.

"We will retreat to the south-west ... here," Blackett explained, as he pointed to the map. "With the Khampas and all of their horses, we'll have the advantage of being more mobile than the reds ... and from tomorrow onwards we'll try to put as much distance between us and them as possible."

Worried expressions on the faces around him gave Blackett reason to pause. He gathered his thoughts and then proceeded to explain himself, "Now that the Chinese have crossed the last major river between here and Lhasa, our main objective will be to keep this guerrilla army intact until we can link up with the remainder of the Tibetan Army ... hopefully that will be in Lhasa ... if it's not already in Chinese hands by that time."

There were looks of concern from the officers, and the Colonel noticed the pain in Phuntsok's eyes at the mention of the capital being captured by the communists. Blackett made an effort to be more positive, "Due to our superior mobility we'll still be able to harass the enemy as he follows us, and cause as much damage as we can without taking significant losses."

"What of the main communist army? Will we attempt to cut across to the south and hinder them ... or send raiding parties to attack their supply lines?" asked Phuntsok.

Blackett admired the Tibetan officer's zeal, and how he was always looking for ways to extend the Khampa's activity to try and slow the Chinese advance on the holy capital. Unfortunately, the CIG colonel had to set aside any emotional perspectives and only approve operations that would not jeopardise the guerrilla army itself and weaken the main body. "I'm afraid that won't be possible Lieutenant. We must get to Lhasa as soon as we can so we can assess the strength of the Tibetan Army there, and then make a determination as to whether the city can be effectively defended."

Ji-zhu's ears pricked at Blackett's last statement. "What if we are too late?" he asked with concern. "Surely we cannot believe that we have been fighting all this time only to fail at the last obstacle?"

Blackett sighed, "Of course we should hope that Lhasa is still in Tibetan hands when we reach it, but we have to be prepared for the worst."

Rhuzkoi knew that many of the Khampas in his unit were almost at the end of their resolve, and with the morale of the lower ranks flagging from the Chinese breakthroughs across the river, it was the job of their chiefs and the officers to bolster the men's spirits. "My brothers, I must admit that when the Bolshevik Red Army was victorious against our Russian Liberation Army in Germany in 1945, that we lost all hope of ever returning to our homeland, or of seeing it freed from their tyranny. As you know, we eventually turned that defeat into victory ... with the help of the Allies."

"Yes!" exclaimed Ji-zhu, "But *we* do not have an Allied army to help us. We are alone up here in this remote mountainous region with only a few airdrops to help keep us in the fight!" The man who had become the Khampa's spiritual leader stood up and faced his brother officers, turning his back on Blackett. "We are seeing our homeland being destroyed by these fanatical invaders! We need to do more than just run away!"

He looked around to Blackett, "I say we should attack the communist army to the south – hit them from the mountains and then keep moving until we can hit them again!"

Blackett raised his arm for silence. "I understand your anguish, but we *need* to maintain our formation – and our strength. We must not weaken ourselves by dividing our army into separate guerrilla units. To take any meaningful action against their main army, we would need to use a battalion-strength force ... and we can't afford to spare that from our main force."

Ji-zhu moved over to the table, lifting a larger scale map from beneath the others and then placing the palm of his hand over Lhasa. He looked Blackett in the eye and spoke in a grave tone, "This is not just some plan on a piece of paper ... this is our home." He waved his hand at his fellow Tibetans, "These men know what losing Lhasa will mean to all Tibetans ... what it will mean if we are defeated and we have no Lhasa – *no Tibet* to return to."

Phuntsok bowed his head. Ji-zhu's words had brought him to the edge of his seat, but now he sat back painfully and put his hand to his chest where the shrapnel was still embedded. Ji-zhu watched his compatriot with a pained expression of his own, and was compelled to add, "Losing our homeland will not just be a loss of territory – of mountains, towns, villages or farms ... and it will not just be a loss for us here, or for all those who now live in Tibet ... it will be a loss for all Tibetans who are to come."

Ji-zhu's eyes pleaded to Blackett for understanding, "We cannot keep retreating, or even think of leaving our country so we can live and fight another day as Colonel Rhuzkoi suggests." He closed his eyes, *there is so much these foreigners do not know about us.*

Blackett raised an eyebrow questioningly, "Why not? You could find refuge in another country like India. The Dalai Llama may already be on his way there to avoid being captured."

Ji-zhu lifted his head, "You may see our meaning one day my friend," he said with resignation. "But for us today, it is different. We are tied to this land in ways you do not understand. Our *souls* are tied to this land. The incarnation of a Tibetan – of all of our people ... depends on the soul being able to return *here* – to Tibet ... not to some other country where we would be separated from the land of our ancestors."

Blackett's blank expression told him that he was wasting his time trying to make someone comprehend what had taken millennia for his own people to realise. He walked toward the doorway to leave, "If we leave now – we may never have a homeland to return to."

As he left, the others silently contemplated his words for a few moments before Lobsang and the other chieftains got up to follow Ji-zhu. Rhuzkoi joined Blackett at the map and the two continued to plan their withdrawal and the next morning's rearguard action.

~ * ~ * ~ * ~

In the near-dark outside the command post, a Tibetan infantryman had been waiting patiently to be allowed entry. Ji-zhu asked him what he wanted, and the soldier told him that Lhasa had radioed for them to expect an important message to be sent at 1900HRS. Ji-zhu checked his watch – the transmission would be in thirty minutes time. He advised Lobsang who went back into the CP to tell Blackett, and then he headed toward the bunker that housed the radio.

On the way there he noticed a Khampa woman tending to some horses. There had been an influx of refugees to the rebel camps, with many women among them. Ji-zhu stopped as though drawn to something unusual about the woman as he watched her. She didn't have the same look about her as the other inhabitants of Kham.

As she filled a horse's feed bag with hay, she noticed him and smiled.

"Is that your horse?" he asked her.

He thought her polished features were possibly Burmese or Malay.

"No, mine is over there. These are the Tibetan Army horses."

She seemed to know who he was and was a little reserved, although still talkative. "I'm just doing what little I can to help around here."

"You are not from Kham are you ... where are you from?" he asked her politely, and he moved to help her.

She finished filling another hay bag from a nearby cart, then stopped to watch Ji-zhu as he carried an armful of hay to the horse in the next roped-off yard. She dusted a few barley husks from her tunic as she answered, "I was not born here, but I now call Tibet my home."

They both took hold of the front shaft of the cart and pulled it further along the row of yards. "My family were traders; my father was Chinese from Hunan and my mother was from Thailand. My parents were killed by bandits while travelling with a caravan along the Tea Road."

"I'm sorry to hear that ... but as we say in Tibet, they will be with you once again."

"Yes, I know ... either here or in the hereafter," she replied with a knowledgeable smile. He thought that when she smiled it told of an inner peace, of a certainty that her parents had simply moved on to another state of being, and that there was no cause for sadness other than that she missed them. Her raven black hair was long, but she had coiled it up in a braid to keep it out of the way while doing chores.

They filled more hay bags and talked as though they had each found someone they immediately felt comfortable with. She sensed that he, just like herself, had a connection to the outside world that most other Tibetans did not have. "I was taken in by a nunnery and began training there."

"Where was that?"

"In Dzogchen monastery. I left when I heard the Chinese were approaching." Her expression saddened for a moment as she added, "I have since heard that the communists set fire to it, and it burned to the ground."

Ji-zhu had heard of many similar incidents and so showed no surprise. As they moved along again, he felt through the shared weight of the cart they were pulling that she was stronger than her slight build suggested. They dropped the shaft in unison and she looked at him. Her eyes danced. It was a momentary flash which awakened a long-forgotten hope in Ji-zhu. She turned from him and took up an armful of hay as she explained, "The life of a nun would not have suited me...and so here I am."

With that single glance she had allowed him to see more than he had ever seen in a woman before. He knew they were kindred spirits and that he wanted to know more about her. "My name is Ji-zhu."

"I know … and I am Fia."

"If you like I will come by and help out again another time."

"I'd like that yes...I'll be here again tomorrow."

"I'm afraid we will be abandoning this camp in the morning – but I'll find you."

As he left her, the glow in his heart was that of a lamp lit once again inside a shrine which had spent years in darkness. His mind reeled with contradictory thoughts as he made his way to the radio bunker. *I must be mad...we're in a war...how can I be thinking of love in a place like this?*

The radio bunker was shrouded with a crude camouflage of foliage cut from the surrounding trees. It was manned by one of the Tibetan infantrymen sitting on a wooden crate wearing a set of earphones. A signal was coming in, and he was diligently writing out the sequences of coded letters. A pause in the transmission allowed the signaller time to push one earpiece back and speak hurriedly to Ji-zhu.

"It is an urgent message from headquarters in Lhasa."

"When you finish decoding it bring it to the command post immediately," said Ji-zhu.

He went back to the CP to ensure that all of the officers were there. Rhuzkoi had already left to organise the rearguard, and Lobsang and the other chieftains were readying the Khampas for the withdrawal in the morning. Blackett and Phuntsok were hovering over the map table once again. The Colonel, who'd received notice of the important signal, was expecting the worst. He was anticipating news that the Chinese were closing in on Lhasa and that the remnants of the Tibetan Army were already pulling out. He looked worried as he and the Lieutenant considered their options. Ji-zhu approached and Blackett asked him, "How long?"

"It is being decoded. Is there anything you need me to do before morning?"

"Yes. Send someone to find Lobsang and have him here for a briefing at 1930. He'll need to pass on any change in plans to the other chiefs."

"Are you expecting new orders from Lhasa?" asked Ji-zhu.

Blackett gave a disconsolate shrug, "They know we're pulling out. They might have other ideas about which direction we should head and what our role will be."

His eyes wandered over the map as though he were searching for some sanctuary to take his army. The setbacks of the previous days had taken their toll on him, and this late in the day lack of sleep was starting to cause deep hollows to form around his eye sockets. "I just hope the news isn't so bad that we have to disband and let the Khampas go back to their farms."

Ji-zhu was taken aback by the Colonel's fears. He'd been thinking that the leadership in Lhasa were as hopeful as he was, and that they might possibly suggest that the Khampas should commence guerrilla attacks on the main Chinese army to their south. Deflated by Blackett's admission, he sat down heavily. Images of the consequences of giving up the fight flooded his mind. After several moments of tortuous speculation, he forced himself not to think about the insanity that would be sure to engulf his country if that were the case.

Phuntsok saw his pain and offered some consolation, even though he was suffering from his own wounds. "Worry not my brother, whatever is to come – they can never touch us in here," he said, putting a symbolic hand on his chest to signify a chamber that harboured his soul.

A call from outside accompanied by running footsteps announced the signaller's arrival. He rushed in and breathlessly handed Blackett the message. The Colonel read it thoughtfully for what seemed like an impossibly long minute to the others.

The Colonel looked up from the paper, shaking his head in disbelief. "They've done it!" he blurted. The angst on his face lifted and his brow uncreased, "The calls for help to the Union of Nations have been answered...and they've sent a relief force from India!"

Ji-zhu sprang up and joined the other two at the table. Blackett replaced the local map with one showing a larger area to the south-east. "Here..." he said as he pointed enthusiastically, "...two days ago, an unopposed airborne landing using gliders and paratroopers...along the floor of the Nyang River valley. From there they are moving north by road up to Nyingchi."

It seemed as though another man was suddenly standing in Blackett's place; the same purposeful man Phuntsok had known in Chamdo from a time that now seemed so long ago. The Colonel saw the looks of pure elation on the faces of the two Tibetans as they reached around the table and gripped each other's arms.

After allowing them a moment to share their joyful release, Blackett stabbed a finger loudly on the map to get their attention. As he traced a line along the route taken by the Indian Army and British paratrooper units, he explained, "Lhasa says they're located at the rear of the Chinese army and are in a position to cut off the enemy's main supply line."

Phuntsok gave Ji-zhu a slap on the back, then held his injured shoulder regretfully. The two Tibetans laughed and looked to Blackett for confirmation of the importance of the news.

He nodded at them, the magnitude of the Security Council's actions taking shape in his mind, and what it meant for their plans. "Yes, my friends, this changes everything."

CHAPTER THIRTY-ONE

"Long Live Ho Chi Minh
The guiding light of the proletariat!
Long live Stalin
The great eternal tree!
Peace grows in his shadow!
Kill, kill again, let your hands never stop
Let fields and paddyfields produce rice in abundance
So that taxes can be paid at once.
Let us march together with the same heart
So that the Party may last for ever
Let us adore Chairman Mao
And build an eternal cult to Stalin"
Nguyen Kim Thanh (To Huu)
Poet and Deputy Prime Minister,
Vietnamese Government

NK 105th Armoured Brigade
Sinuiju,
North Korea
July 15th, 1949

The long brown stripe of the Yalu River flowed inexorably toward the Yellow Sea, carrying tree branches and other flotsam picked up during recent rainstorms.

General Yong-nam watched in isolated silence from the northern bank of the river as his armoured brigade continued its retreat across the Yalu and into Manchuria. The tanks, trucks and armoured troop carriers didn't appear as though they'd been battered by continuous battle, but instead looked like they had just rolled out of the factories in China.

Replacements, he thought, *it is no wonder we have not been able to stand our ground...plenty of new equipment but not enough experienced soldiers to use it.*

He thought of the futility of the previous month's fighting. As a commander, he would have deeply shamed by the performance of the North Korean armies, had he not been secretly hoping for an outcome such as this. The loss of life and destruction of materiel had been on a staggering scale. The overwhelming firepower of the Allied artillery and tanks on the ground, and from their dominant air cover, had eventually worn down the defensive capability of the communists.

His ongoing duplicity to deceive the communists had been resulting in a contradictory state of mind, so much so that at times he had to find an hour of solitude just so he could refocus his concentration.

The Chinese have kept up a continuous supply of tanks and artillery, he thought as he tried to put the situation into a clearer perspective ... *and they have even begun to provide reinforcements to our depleted NK divisions, but without committing their own ground formations.*

The General scanned the sky. The dark clouds that had delivered the hours of morning rain were dispersing as noon approached. He glanced back at the railway bridge. It had taken the Chinese engineers the whole of the previous day and much of the night to get it converted for road traffic by laying specially cut timbers over the top of the rails. For the first few hours after it had become ready, only wheeled vehicles and soldiers on foot had been allowed to cross to avoid any congestion. Now, the armoured vehicles were joining the procession, but they were moving very slowly so they didn't damage the improvised surface with their tracks.

Anxiety welled up within Yong-nam as he sensed the threat posed by the clearing weather to the painfully slow-moving column.

If it is already cloudless over the Allies' side of the river, then it will not be long before they send their bombers.

His mind once again clarified, he decided to return to his headquarters command post. He turned away from the river and walked a short distance through the trees to a large concrete bunker. As the General went into his private quarters, Major Kee followed behind him and saluted. "General, our artillery battalion has now been reinforced by two companies of 85mm anti-aircraft guns," he advised as he read from a clipboard. "... and their crews are Chinese."

Yong-nam just nodded. The two officers were alone so he didn't have to make any effort to show that he cared. Major Kee put down the board with its thick sheaf of casualty reports and other papers, "We are also to receive a visit from our newly assigned CCP advisor."

"When?"

Kee looked at his watch, "In fifteen minutes."

Yong-nam cursed. "This will be typical behaviour from our communist overlords now that we are on Chinese soil," he lamented angrily. "No doubt they will expect us to be grateful they gave us any warning at all."

He looked searchingly at Kee. The two had a bond of trust that went deeper than their sharing the dangers of battle. It was more so from their clandestine activities to undermine the communists. "Are the other officers ready? Do we need to brief them, or can they be trusted not to give our guest any cause to begin snooping?"

Kee didn't have to think about his response. It was his job to ensure that the cadre of officers working with them were always kept informed of any developments. "They will have been prepared. I sent Lieutenant Ban to make his rounds as soon the message came through this morning. Our men will not need to explain to the Chinese why we have been retreating – they are aware of the demand the North Korean Army received from Mao, and I have instructed our officers to use the term *strategic withdrawal*."

Yong-nam signified his approval, "Good. Have a suitably modest lunch brought in...I do not want our CCP advisor to think we are suffering any less than our men are."

Thirty minutes later the CCP officer, Shang Wei Shen arrived. His uniform was a plain olive-green tunic over breeches, with a drab brown cap. Yong-nam recognised the attire as representative of the peasant-style appearance that the Chinese Communist Party had been conveying to their people. However, the Korean was immune to the intended sympathetic influence of the Shang Wei's uniform, and knew it was a crude attempt to reassure the Chinese people that the military arm of the Party was in some way acting in their interests.

Yong-nam's gut burned at the hypocrisy, as he had been receiving intelligence reports on how many millions of Chinese peasants had been killed at the hands of the Party's collectivist policies.

He suppressed his rage and the indignation of being kept waiting by a lower ranked officer, as he issued a polite welcome. "Shang Wei Shen...welcome to the 105th Armoured Brigade. You are late. We trust you found our headquarters without too much difficulty?"

Shen ignored the invitation to apologise for his lateness. His expression remained expressionless. It was a mask that conveyed contempt and moral superiority. "General Yong-nam, it is I who am welcoming you...to the territory of the nation which has supported Korea's struggle to rid its land of the foreign imperialists."

Yong-nam stood motionless, aware that although Shen's rank was lower than his own, it was through him that the CCP's power would now be emanating here. The Shang Wei acknowledged Kee with a nod and moved to the table laden with a simple fare of fish, rice and pickled vegetables. As he filled his bowl, he spoke over his shoulder at the two North Koreans. "Our great Chairman Mao has tasked the armies in this sector with the responsibility of ensuring the westerners are not merely halted at our border...but pushed back to Kunsan and into the sea from which they were disgorged."

Yong-nam remained silent. He knew he had to hold his tongue and not provoke the Party's representative by voicing any doubts about the Chinese strategy, however unrealistic it may be.

The Sheng Wei shovelled a few mouthfuls of food into his mouth before continuing. "Chairman Mao has spoken to your revolutionary leaders and informed them of the role he expects North Korea to play in order to correct the unfortunate predicament you have gotten yourselves into."

Yong-nam bristled but persisted in keeping his temper in check.

Shen continued as though he were addressing a pair of subordinates, "I will attempt to accurately convey the Chairman's exact words when he spoke with your Kim Il Sung in Peking...that the liberation of your country will have to be temporarily forsaken so that you may contribute more substantially to the greater cause of China's global communist revolution."

Another mouthful kept Yong-nam and Kee waiting attentively. "The Chairman generously assured Kim that his armies have not lost face in the eyes of the Chinese people."

Deeply insulted, Yong-nam had no response at his disposal other than to bow slightly. He didn't care how the Chinese perceived him; the success of his ultimate mission would justify any pretence he now showed to the CCP.

Shen put down the bowl, "As for the immediate situation, high command has ordered that the bridge over the Yalu at Sinuiju must remain intact so that it can be used for a counter-offensive. Your men must fight to the death here to stop the enemy getting across...until reinforcements can arrive. Do you have any questions regarding these orders?"

The General remained silent.

"Good. Then perhaps now we can discuss your plans for the defence of your sector in more detail. How soon will your brigade have completed its crossing?"

Major Kee answered on the General's behalf, trying to spare him any further indignity. "We expect to have our units deployed for the defence of the northern side of the river by nightfall tomorrow. A rearguard will withdraw from Sinuiju tomorrow night."

"That plan will hardly be sufficient, but it will have to do for now," Shen said with measured scorn. "Considering the plight that Korea now finds itself in – I will now share the information I have been authorised to pass on to you. Chairman Mao, in his wisdom, has seen fit to commit three of our armies...one hundred thousand men, to repel any westerners from our Korean border."

Shen waited for a reaction from Yong-nam, but the North Korean General didn't flinch. Shen thought it strange, almost as if the General was trying not to show his true feelings. He made a mental note of it and then continued.

"The decision to send these ground forces has been a difficult one considering the situation on China's northern border with Russia – we would have sent more troops, but they may be needed for our own defence. So...forward units of the 40th Field Army under General Chin Teh-huai will be arriving here tomorrow. You will make your brigade available to him as soon as he has established his headquarters. Is that understood?"

Yong-nam heard the Chinese General's name with a shudder. Chin Teh-huai was a fanatic, renowned for having no regard for the lives of his men. Tens of thousands off communist soldiers had perished under his command during the Chinese civil war. He would almost certainly be sending the lowly North Koreans into the heaviest of the fighting and ordering them to fight to the death.

Yong-nam was too weary to make any objections, or to contrive some reason for getting his brigade diverted to the rear in a reserve role away from the fighting. He simply nodded.

"Good. Now, please join me" said Shen, waving his chopsticks at the table.

Yong-nam raised the effort to keep his emotions under control, "If you will excuse me...I have no appetite, and also have other duties to attend to. Major Kee will escort you on your tour of our defences."

With that polite rebuttal he walked toward the exit, ignoring Shen as he snapped out a brisk salute. He may have to submit to the CCP's will through this bureaucrat wearing a uniform, but he would not dignify such an officer with any military courtesy. As a career military man forced to conduct himself in what he considered to be a dishonourable

manner due to yet another war brought on by political motivations, his distrust of politicians was growing into a deep-
seated hatred.

Once outside he walked disconsolately away from the
meeting and into the trees. Out of sight of the sentries, he
sat on a log beneath a tree, shaking with anger. He needed
to be away from the war for a while to allow himself to think.
He couldn't rely on getting any peace in his quarters as he
was sure to be interrupted. Clasping his hands together in
front of his face, he tried to wring out his frustration. His
thoughts were in turmoil. How were he and his cadre of officers supposed to continue to covertly fight the communists,
and to undermine them from within now that his brigade
was to be under the direct command of the Chinese 40th
Field Army? How could he best serve his fellow Koreans'
goal of achieving re-unification? He thought long and hard,
only beginning to see the course they would need to take
more clearly once he'd shut out the world around him.

Only *he* would be able to ensure that his officers and the
men of his brigade were not to be treated as cannon fodder.
He needed to continue on, showing complete obedience to
the Party, but manoeuvring tactically to try to prevent the
slaughter which he knew the CCP's directives would bring
about.

He took solace from a story that the Russian officer,
Rhuzkoi, had told him...of General Vlasov and his renegade
army who had fought against Stalin's Red Army – their own
countrymen. *At least they won in the end...but at such a great
cost to their own. We Koreans are in a different situation, and
the time is not yet right to try to convince all of the men in
our brigade that we should join the Union of Nations
forces...but where there is hope there can still be victory.*

The sound of anti-aircraft guns brough the world around him back into focus and confirmed his earlier fears. He strained to see through the trees as he headed for the riverbank. Black puffs dotted the sky at high altitude, and all around him soldiers were running for cover. Yong-nam strode up to a freshly dug trench between two commercial buildings five hundred yards downstream from the bridge.

Two infantrymen who had been huddled in the bottom of the trench, cowering, stood rigidly to attention at the sight of the general standing over them. Yong-nam lowered his hand signalling them to at-ease, then raised his field-glasses skyward. Thousands of feet above, the silver flecks of Allied bombers approached resolutely from the east, following the distinctive line of the river to their target – the bridge. He switched his view further to the north where a swirling pattern of white contrails twisted their way toward the bombers. Jet fighters from both sides in a desperate dogfight; Chinese MiGs trying to claw their way through a screen of USAF Sabres.

Black smoke trails marked where several jets had been downed, but it was too far away for the General to see which side they belonged to. The criss-cross lines of vapour moved slowly closer to the straight lines of the bombers' own contrails, telling Yong-nam that some of the MiGs must be getting through. He may have been insulated and impartial toward the overall tide of the conflict between the communists and the Union of Nations in the Far East, but as he glanced down at the hundreds of his troops and dozens of vehicles caught in the open on the bridge, he felt a pang of despair.

If any of the brigade are trapped on the other side, then the Chinese order to fight to the last man will be their death sentence.

As the first wave of planes began dropping their bombs onto the NK positions on both sides of the river, Yong-nam looked up and saw a bright orange flash among the distant silver-grey shapes. *The MiGs have scored a kill*, he thought with indifference. But the dozens more of the slowly moving flecks told him that nearly all the Allied force would soon be over the target zone.

Huge explosions and billowing smoke began to devour the small town of Sinuiju and grew louder as the bombs crept closer to Yong-nam. A line of enormous muddy water-spouts sprang up from the Yalu, straddling the bridge. Panicked soldiers ran desperately to try and get off the bomber's main target, some leaping into the murky water in the hope they would be carried downstream to safety.

The two soldiers near Yong-nam dropped down and flattened themselves against the bottom of their trench as the shattering blasts of high-explosive clamoured ever closer.

Buildings dissolved in clouds of dust and debris along the street, and the heated shockwaves threatened to bowl the General over, but he kept his stance. His gaze was fixed determinedly on the bridge as the Black Dragon's breath consumed the air about him...but this was no dream. He closed his eyes, in the hope that shutting out the destruction around him might thwart the falling bombs from finding their mark. Long and fateful seconds passed, the fiery air depriving his lungs of oxygen and almost causing him to pass out. When he was finally able to take a gasp of air, he opened his eyes to look at the bridge, then exhaled with dread.

An obscuring wall of muddy spray and smoke drifted away to reveal a hundred-foot gap where one span of the bridge had just plunged into the Yalu. A despondent Yong-nam took a few steps and then put out an arm to lean against the solid support of a telegraph pole. He knew that many hundreds of lives, a third of his brigade, would now be lost due to orders from General Chin Teh-huai to fight to the last man.

Perhaps those less indoctrinated to communism will mutiny...shoot some of their die-hard officers and allow themselves to be captured by the Allies, he thought, but he knew it was only wishful thinking.

He left the scene of devastation behind him and went to find Major Kee so they could begin to revise their defensive planning and prepare for the war of attrition that was to come.

CHAPTER THIRTY-TWO

Mojave City
2268 CE

"Hesta please begin," instructed Arjon as he donned his Immerser.

The Tibetan sky was clear and bright, a deceptive contrast to the cloud of evil which was blackening the land beneath it.

The alternative history of Tibet flooded Arjon's consciousness. In this other world, the Chinese had taken Lhasa. After failing to win control over the inhabitants by manipulating the National Assembly, they were now crushing all resistance with brute force.

A figure materialised into the simulation beside him, and he was prompted to provide a warning before the full mental synchronisation kicked in.

"Coralex, try to keep it in the back of your mind that this is a simulation. The horrors we may witness did not occur in our own past," he advised as they began walking along a steep mountain path.

"I'm ready. I've been given further psychological training with the Immerser to bolster my mental defences against the impact of seeing the atrocities here."

"Oh? How did you achieve that?...aversion therapy by experiencing documentaries of ancient Rome under Caligula?"

"No, they were episodes from a series of experimental spiritual exercises I uploaded from the Directory's library. They included meditations to help me re-focus on the positive state of mind of my non-sim existence while integrated within an alternative reality. If you see me close my eyes periodically it's because I'm trying to reconnect to the memories of my happy place."

Arjon hoped Hesta was taking note so that he could request a copy of the exercises for himself, hoping they might be successful at alleviating the post-sim trauma he'd been inflicted with following his previous Immerser sessions.

The mountain air was brisk even under the direct sunlight, and as their senses became more engulfed in their environment, the pair's utopian memories soon faded. A short while later they rounded a switchback and a Khampa sentry stepped out from behind a large boulder. He raised his rifle warily at them, "Who are you?"

"I'm Arjon, and this is Coralex...we are from India."

"Why are you up here?" The tribesman wasn't going to let them continue up the path unless they provided valid a reason according to the logical bounds of the matrix.

"We bring news of the Dalai Llama. We wish to speak with Ji-zhu."

The sentry looked them over with a scowl and then reluctantly waved them through. As the strangers walked past him, he stepped forward to confirm that no-one was coming up the trail behind them.

The two hiked a short distance before they reached a campsite comprising a few tents spread out under a stand of trees that marked the edge of the treeline. Further up the slope, bare brown rocks and rubble continued on up to the snow-capped peak. Several Khampas were resting by a small fire, and some of them appeared to be injured.

Further along they saw Ji-zhu sitting in his tent and writing in a journal. He looked up and saw them approaching so he got up and walked out of from under the open tent-flap. He recognised them as the visitors from India he'd previously met at the monastery in the valley far below. He beckoned for them to take a seat around the smouldering remains of his campfire. His left hand was bandaged.

"You've been hurt!" said Coralex with dismay.

"It is just a bullet graze...there was a firefight at the monastery. The monks had refused to leave so I gathered together a group of Khampas from the mountains and we returned to the monastery to try to stop the Chinese from butchering the monks. We arrived too late...and we took many casualties. The few of us here are all that survived."

"What will you do now?" asked Arjon.

"The communists are searching these mountains for us. We will have to move again shortly."

"We'll only stay for a short while," said Arjon. "We have heard from India that the Dalai Llama's efforts to find a peaceful solution to the war have been thwarted, and he has been persuaded that the only chance of saving Tibetan culture is for your people to find sanctuary by joining him in India."

Ji-zhu nodded, "We knew as much. The Khampas in the mountains will continue their fight and will be planning how to stop the Chinese from preventing any Tibetans from leaving."

"What will you do next?" asked Coralex.

"Keep fighting...keep moving – the Khampas will never give up. They believe they can hold out in the mountains for years."

"But what about you?" Coralex pleaded, "You're not a Khampa – you could escape to India too. There's so much you could do for the Tibetans in exile."

"They will not need me," Ji-zhu replied solemnly. "But if they leave, I fear for their future in a new land to which they hold no connection."

The sage grimaced and looked up toward the summit, "The most that any of us can do is to ensure that no-one forgets what has happened here," he said forlornly. "One day these crimes will be accounted for – though I doubt that any of us here will be witness to it."

Coralex closed her eyes. Arjon thought for a moment that she was meditating to help block out the images of murdered monks or nuns being raped, but then he saw tears flowing down her cheeks. She opened her eyes again and looked at Ji-zhu.

"Is that why you're writing in that journal? You've given up...and you think that leaving a record of what you've seen is all that you can do?"

Ji-zhu glared at her, "The Chinese communists are monsters!" he spat vehemently. "To look into their eyes is to look into the blackness of a void! They commit atrocities in the name of some deceitful revolution...but they kill without conscience – with no thought for those people of goodwill they are conquering...but only for the future of their own pointless existence!"

Arjon and Coralex sat in frozen silence, shocked by the anger in Ji-zhu's voice and the yearning for vengeance on his face. The Tibetan continued to vent the emotions from which he had no other avenue for relief. "If they are allowed to go unpunished then it will be a damning indictment on the whole human race!"

Arjon sighed sympathetically, "Yes...of course you are right." From his enlightened perspective he knew that what the Chinese were doing was simply the conclusion to a story that had been played out by humans for millennia. It was the extreme manifestation of the maddening human compulsion to tell other people what they can or cannot do, and then forcing them to be the same as they are.

"They should be punished..." he said grimly, "...and not just the Chinese – but anyone who unjustly imposes their will upon others. The crimes here are not limited to atrocities against Tibetans but are inflicted on the entire human race...that's why they are called 'crimes against humanity'...and as such it is a testament to the ineptitude of your United Nations."

Coralex's irritation with this insane version of the Earth had been growing as she'd been sitting and listening, and she'd been caught up in Ji-zhu's frustration with the lack of a response from the other countries of his world. She could sense the tragedy of the United Nation's inability to intervene in Tibet.

"Pah! They are nothing but a pillar of appeasement!" she said angrily. "They are a trivial platform for all of the conflicting ideologies that have sprung up like a pestilence on this corrupted Earth."

Arjon turned toward her, surprised at her outburst and concerned her words may be infringing on the logical bounds of the simulation, "Coralex...we're not supposed to..."

"She is right!" Ji-zhu stated emphatically. "Cultures such as the Chinese that have embraced evil and are then allowed to propagate it without being contained – are a cancer! They are an infection that will consume the spirit of personal liberty of the free peoples of the Earth." He looked to the cold, grey ashes of the fire pit before them, "If it were up to me, I would put every single one of them in a hole...a very deep, very dark hole."

Coralex was pained to see such a tolerant and peaceful man suffering from the struggle between his good nature and the wrath caused by the injustices around him.

A silent anguish hung over the trio as they each stared into the warm ashes of the dying campfire. It was as though they were hoping a blazing flame of redemption would suddenly burst forth and overcome their hopelessness.

As though answering a call to rescue the deeply depressed utopians, Hesta intervened. She had contacted Thiessen who was travelling in his air-car, and after filling him in had asked him to join his colleagues in their Immerser session.

The CoT field agent blithely walked into the campsite as though it were an expected consequence of the situation.

"Thiessen!" Arjon cried in disbelief, "...but how?"

Thiessen sat down and explained, "I told the sentry that I was keeping watch for the Chinese further down the mountain." He turned to Ji-zhu, "They are not far behind me and will soon find this camp."

Arjon introduced Thiessen as another member of their party from India, and then advised Ji-zhu, "You should leave this mountain now."

The Tibetan cast a rebellious eye over the group of foreigners, letting out a soft chuckle, "We are pitifully few, but we will make the communists pay in blood for every inch of this mountain."

"But what if you can't fight them off?" asked a desperate Coralex. "Your journal...no-one will ever see it!"

Ji-zhu shrugged, "If it is not from my own words then the testimony of those who survive will have the same effect."

Thiessen's eyes lit up at the mention of the journal and he asked if he could see it. Ji-zhu retrieved it from the tent, and the CoT agent was surprised it was not written in Sanskrit but in English.

As Thiessen skimmed over the pages Ji-zhu explained, "My travels in India have shown me the far-reaching extent of British influence. It made sense to leave an account in their language."

A short time later they noticed the Khampa sentry return to the camp and warn his kinsmen of the approaching Chinese. Ji-zhu issued a series of quick instructions for them to break camp, and then asked for the return of the journal from Thiessen. "You should go now. There is a goat path behind us which leads back down the mountain."

The visitors left, and once out of sight of the camp Hesta started to decrease the intensity of their synaptic connections to their Immersers. They each became more aware of their utopian existence but remained in a half-realised awareness of the simulation's surroundings. It was a way of easing the transition between the two realities.

Each of them harboured uncertain thoughts as to whether they would see Ji-zhu again, or if there would be anything further they could learn from this chapter of the simulation. An emotionally drained Coralex took her leave and disconnected. Arjon took Thiessen's arm and asked him to stay in the matrix with him. As they clambered down the rough path, stumbling along on its gravelly surface, Arjon spoke to Thiessen about Ji-zhu's journal. "Perhaps this book is something that has existed in both realities. If Ji-zhu was inclined to write things down, then he may have left something behind in our own world."

He stopped in his tracks, struck by a significant possibility, "That may explain something of how Hesta formulated Ji-zhu's character...from some remnants of his journal which were somehow uploaded to the meganet."

Thiessen stopped a few paces ahead, and turned back to face Arjon, "I believe you may have something there – I will continue my investigations with that in mind."

With that they parted ways, leaving the insanity of the Tibetan genocide behind them as they gratefully returned to their own reality.

EPILOGUE

"To be no more: sad cure! For who would lose,
Though full of pain, this intellectual being,
Those thoughts that wander through eternity,
To perish rather, swallowed up and lost
In the wide womb of uncreated night,
Devoid of sense and motion?"

John Milton
Paradise Lost

This verse from Milton's Paradise Lost echoes to us from centuries past. The lines are spoken by a voice of evil, Belial, who had been cast down into Hell alongside Satan. Belial was speaking against Satan's call for a war against what he and his cohorts perceived to be the oppression of a higher power.

Our history shows that the Russian and Chinese communists were in a similar situation in 1950. With the Soviets having just acquired the A-Bomb, and the Chinese having defeated Chiang Kai-shek's Nationalists in their civil war – the communists, just like Belial, saw their existence under threat from a stronger foe: the West.

In hindsight, it was inevitable the communists would take advantage of any opportunity to start another war. That opportunity soon came in Korea, not long after a fateful statement by the U.S. Secretary of State, Dean Acheson which described the West's defensive perimeter in Asia with the glaring omission of any mention of the Korean peninsula.

The exclusion of Korea when it was announced, could almost be seen as confirmation by Washington that it would be unable to effectively contain the spread of communism in the region, or be able to defend the Koreans if the communists attacked, which they duly did on June 25th, 1950.

The rest is history – our history, as depicted by Hesta's simulations.

Contrastingly, in the utopian history where the Free World War continues on from the defeat of the Soviets, the Chinese communists have obtained the A-Bomb from the renegade dictator Stalin. Would the CCP be so emboldened by its possession that they would take on the rest of the world?

In the Russian Far East, the Allies have intervened at the request of President Vlasov's Russian Republic. The North Koreans have been pushed back across the Yalu River and into China by superior Allied forces. Similarly, in Tibet, the Allies have sent a relief force to try and counter the Chinese invasion and looming genocide.

These scenarios in the utopian world are only possible because of the Soviet defeat in the Free World War. This was due to General Patton's influence which would have facilitated a continuation of readiness to deter the threat of global communism. The same maintenance of armed forces, levels of production and superiority of arms by the West would have been required to contain the Chinese communists two years later.

All of these events undertaken by the Allies could only have been sanctioned by a Union of Nations Charter which decreed that certain basic human rights should be protected. Rights to individual liberties that stem from the fundamental democratic privilege of the people *to vote*, and subsequently remove from office those who abuse their power or who are unfit to direct the lives of others.

It is highly probable that the communists facing such a threat would see their predicament in the same light as Milton saw that of the satanic hosts contained in Hell. It is likely the CCP leadership, driven by paranoia, fear, arrogance and the desire to retain absolute authority over their own people would seek to alter the balance of global power no matter what the cost in lives...or even at the risk of 'being swallowed up and lost in the wide womb of uncreated night'.

There would be a very high probability of evil.

COMING SOON!

The final instalment of this series, "The Free World War III: The Sealed Globe", builds further on the concept of simulations produced by probability algorithms and machine learning. It reveals in greater depth, the world of Arjon and Eya, and the events that led to the founding of their utopian society. It also brings to a dramatic conclusion, the war to free the world from tyranny and perpetual conflict.

ABOUT THE AUTHOR

Matthew W. Frend is a computer programmer who has lived in Australia, USA and Scotland. He lives by the Benjamin Franklin credo of "Either write something worth reading or do something worth writing".

A diverse background includes time spent in the Australian Army and 20 years in Information Technology.

Outside of work, he has been involved with equestrian sports at the grass roots level and enjoys cycling.

Printed in Great Britain
by Amazon

66692653R00149